BELIEVE ME

Books by Tahereh Mafi

The Shatter Me Series
Shatter Me
Unravel Me
Ignite Me
Restore Me
Defy Me
Imagine Me

Novellas
Destroy Me
Fracture Me
Shadow Me
Reveal Me
Believe Me

Novella Collections
Unite Me
Find Me

This Woven Kingdom
An Emotion of Great Delight
A Very Large Expanse of Sea
Furthermore
Whichwood

BELIEVE ME

TAHEREH MAFI

HARPER

An Imprint of HarperCollinsPublishers

ONE

The wall is unusually white.

More white than is usual. Most people think white walls are true white, but the truth is, they only seem white and are not actually white. Most shades of white are mixed in with a bit of yellow, which helps soften the harsh edges of a pure white, making it more of an ecru, or ivory. Various shades of cream. Egg white, even. True white is practically intolerable as a color, so white it's nearly blue.

This wall, in particular, is not so white as to be offensive, but a sharp enough shade of white to pique my curiosity, which is nothing short of a miracle, really, because I've been staring at it for the greater part of an hour. Thirty-seven minutes, to be exact.

I am being held hostage by custom. Formality.

"Five more minutes," she says. "I promise."

I hear the rustle of fabric. Zippers. A shudder of—

"Is that tulle?"

"You're not supposed to be listening!"

"You know, love, it occurs to me now that I've lived through hostage situations less torturous than this."

"Okay, okay, it's off. Packed away. I just need a second to put on my cl—"

"That won't be necessary," I say, turning around. "Surely this part, I should be allowed to watch."

I lean against the unusually white wall, studying her as she frowns at me, her lips still parted around the shape of a word she seems to have forgotten.

"Please continue," I say, gesturing with a nod. "Whatever you were doing before."

She holds on to her frown for a moment longer than is honest, her eyes narrowing in a show of frustration that is pure fraud. She compounds this farce by clutching an article of clothing to her chest, feigning modesty.

I do not mind, not one single bit.

I drink her in, her soft curves, her smooth skin. Her hair is beautiful at any length, but it's been longer lately. Long and rich, silky against her skin, and—when I'm lucky—against mine.

Slowly, she drops the shirt.

I stand up straighter.

"I'm supposed to wear this under the dress," she says, her fake anger already forgotten. She fidgets with the boning of a cream-colored corset, her fingers lingering along the garter belt, the lace-trimmed stockings. She can't meet my eyes. She's gone shy, and this time, it's real.

Do you like it?

The unspoken question.

I assumed, when she invited me into this dressing room, that it was for reasons beyond me staring at the color variations in an unusually white wall. I assumed she wanted me here to see something.

To see her.

I see now that I was correct.

"You are so beautiful," I say, unable to shed the awe in my voice. I hear it, the childish wonder in my tone, and it embarrasses me more than it should. I know I shouldn't be ashamed to feel deeply. To be moved.

Still, I feel awkward.

Young.

Quietly, she says, "I feel like I just spoiled the surprise. You're not supposed to see any of this until the wedding night."

My heart actually stops for a moment.

The wedding night.

She closes the distance between us and twines her arms around me, freeing me from my momentary paralysis. My heart beats faster with her here, so close. And though I don't know how she knew that I suddenly required the reassurance of her touch, I'm grateful. I exhale, pulling her fully against me, our bodies relaxing, remembering each other.

I press my face into her hair, breathe in the sweet scent of her shampoo, her skin. It's only been two weeks. Two weeks since the end of an old world. The beginning of a new one.

She still feels like a dream to me.

"Is this really happening?" I whisper.

A sharp knock at the door startles my spine straight.

Ella frowns at the sound. "Yes?"

"So sorry to bother you right now, miss, but there's a gentleman here wishing to speak with Mr. Warner."

Ella and I lock eyes.

"Okay," she says quickly. "Don't be mad."

"Why would I be mad?"

Ella pulls away to better look me in the eye. Her own eyes are bright, beautiful. Full of concern. "It's Kenji."

I force down a spike of anger so violent I think I give myself a stroke. "What is he doing here?" I manage to get out. "How did he know how to find us?"

She bites her lip. "We took Amir and Olivier with us."

"I see." We took extra guards along, which means our outing was posted to the public security bulletin. Of course.

Ella nods. "He found me just before we left. He was worried—he wanted to know why we were heading back into the old regulated lands."

I try to say something then, to marvel aloud at Kenji's inability to make a simple deduction despite the abundance of contextual clues right before his eyes—but she holds up a finger.

"I told him," she says, "that we were looking for replacement outfits and reminded him that, for now, the Supply Centers are still the only places to shop for food or clothing or"—she waves a hand, frowns—"anything, at the moment. Anyway, he said he'd try to meet us here. He said he wanted to help."

My eyes widen slightly. I feel another stroke incoming. "He said he wanted to *help*."

She nods.

"Astonishing." A muscle ticks in my jaw. "And funny, too, because he's already helped so much—just last night he helped us both a great deal by destroying my suit and your dress, forcing us to now purchase clothing from a"—I look around, gesture at nothing—"a *store* on the very day we're supposed to get married."

"Aaron," she whispers. She steps closer again. Places a hand on my chest. "He feels terrible about it."

"And you?" I say, studying her face, her feelings. "Don't *you* feel terrible about it? Alia and Winston worked so hard to make you something beautiful, something designed precisely for you—"

"I don't mind." She shrugs. "It's just a dress."

"But it was your wedding dress," I say, my voice failing me now.

She sighs, and in the sound I hear her heart break, more for me than for herself. She turns around and unzips the massive garment bag hanging on a hook above her head.

"You're not supposed to see this," she says, tugging yards of tulle out of the bag, "but I think it might mean more to you than it does to me, so"—she turns back, smiles—"I'll let you help me decide what to wear tonight."

I nearly groan aloud at the reminder.

A nighttime wedding. Who on earth is married at night? Only the hapless. The unfortunate. Though I suppose we

5

now count among their ranks.

Rather than reschedule the entire thing, we pushed it a few hours so that we'd have time to purchase new clothes. Well, I have clothes. My clothes don't matter as much.

But her dress. He destroyed her dress the night before our wedding. Like a monster.

I'm going to murder him.

"You can't murder him," she says, still pulling handfuls of fabric out of the bag.

"I'm certain I said no such thing out loud."

"No," she says, "but you were thinking it, weren't you?"

"Wholeheartedly."

"You can't murder him," she says simply. "Not now. Not ever."

I sigh.

She's still struggling to unearth the gown.

"Forgive me, love, but if all this"—I nod at the garment bag, the explosion of tulle—"is for a single dress, I'm afraid I already know how I feel about it."

She stops tugging. Turns around, eyes wide. "You don't like it? You haven't even seen it yet."

"I've seen enough to know that whatever this is, it's not a gown. This is a haphazard layering of polyester." I lean around her, pinching the fabric between my fingers. "Do they not carry silk tulle in this store? Perhaps we can speak to the seamstress."

"They don't have a seamstress here."

"This is a clothing store," I say. I turn the bodice inside out, frowning at the stitches. "Surely there must be a seamstress. Not a very good one, clearly, but—"

"These dresses are made in a factory," she says to me. "Mostly by machine."

I straighten.

"You know, most people didn't grow up with private tailors at their disposal," she says, a smile playing at her lips. "The rest of us had to buy clothes off the rack. Premade. Ill-fitting."

"Yes," I say stiffly. I feel suddenly stupid. "Of course. Forgive me. The dress is very nice. Perhaps I should wait for you to try it on. I gave my opinion too hastily."

For some reason, my response only makes things worse.

She groans, shooting me a single, defeated look before folding herself into the little dressing room chair.

My heart plummets.

She drops her face in her hands. "It really is a disaster, isn't it?"

Another swift knock at the door. "Sir? The gentleman seems very eager t—"

"He's certainly not a gentleman," I say sharply. "Tell him to wait."

A moment of hesitation. Then, quietly: "Yes, sir."

"Aaron."

I don't need to look up to know that she's unhappy with my rudeness. The owners of this particular Supply Center shut down their entire store for us, and they've been excruciatingly kind. I know I'm being an ass. At present, I can't seem to help it.

"*Aaron.*"

"Today is your wedding day," I say, unable to meet her eyes. "He has ruined your wedding day. Our wedding day."

She gets to her feet. I feel her frustration fade. Transform. Shuffle through sadness, happiness, hope, fear, and finally—

Resignation.

One of the worst possible feelings on what should be a joyous day. Resignation is worse than frustration. Far worse.

My anger calcifies.

"He hasn't ruined it," she says finally. "We can still make this work."

"You're right," I say, pulling her into my arms. "Of course you're right. It doesn't matter, really. None of it does."

"But it's my wedding day," she says. "And I have nothing to wear."

"You're right." I kiss the top of her head. "I'm going to kill him."

A sudden pounding at the door.

I stiffen. Spin around.

"Hey, guys?" More pounding. "I know you're super pissed at me, but I have good news, I swear. I'm going to fix this. I'm going to make it up to you."

I'm just about to respond when Ella tugs at my hand, silencing my scathing retort with a single motion. She shoots me a look that plainly says—

Give him a chance.

I sigh as the anger settles inside my body, my shoulders dropping with the weight of it. Reluctantly, I step aside to allow her to deal with this idiot in the manner she prefers.

It is her wedding day, after all.

Ella steps closer to the door. Points at it, jabbing her finger at the unusually white paint as she speaks. "This better be good, Kenji, or Warner is going to kill you, and I'm going to help him do it."

And then, just like that—

I'm smiling again.

TWO

We're driven back to the Sanctuary the same way we're driven everywhere these days—in a black, all-terrain, bullet-proof SUV—but the car and its heavily tinted windows only make us more conspicuous, which I find worrisome. But then, as Castle likes to point out, I have no ready solution for the problem, so we remain at an impasse.

I try to hide my reaction as we drive up through the wooded area just outside the Sanctuary, but I can't help my grimace or the way my body locks down, preparing for a fight. After the fall of The Reestablishment, most rebel groups emerged from hiding to rejoin the world—

But not us.

Just last week we cleared this dirt path for the SUV, enabling it to now get as close as possible to the unmarked entrance, but I'm not sure it's doing much to help. A mob of people has already crowded in so tightly around us that we're moving no more than an inch at a time. Most of them are well-meaning, but they scream and pound at the car with the enthusiasm of a belligerent crowd, and every time we endure this circus I have to physically force myself to remain calm. To sit quietly in my seat and ignore the urge to remove the gun from its holster beneath my jacket.

Difficult.

I know Ella can protect herself—she's proven this fact a thousand times over—but still, I can't help but worry. She's become notorious to a near-terrifying degree. To some extent, we all have. But Juliette Ferrars, as she's known around the world, can go nowhere and do nothing without drawing a crowd.

They say they love her.

Even so, we remain cautious. There are still many around the globe who would love to bring back to life the emaciated remains of The Reestablishment, and assassinating a beloved hero would be the most effective start to such a scheme. Though we have unprecedented levels of privacy in the Sanctuary, where Nouria's sight and sound protections around the grounds grant us freedoms we enjoy nowhere else, we've been unable to hide our precise location. People know, generally, where to find us, and that small bit of information has been feeding them for weeks. The civilians wait here—thousands and thousands of them—every single day.

For no more than a glimpse.

We've had to put barricades in place. We've had to hire extra security, recruiting armed soldiers from the local sectors. This area is unrecognizable from what it was a month ago. It's a different world already. And I feel my body go solid as we approach the entrance. Nearly there now.

I look up, ready to say something—

"Don't worry." Kenji locks eyes with me. "Nouria upped the security. There should be a team of people waiting for us."

"I don't know why all this is necessary," Ella says, still staring out the window. "Why can't I just stop for a minute and talk to them?"

"Because the last time you did that you were nearly trampled," Kenji says, exasperated.

"Just the one time."

Kenji's eyes go wide with outrage, and on this point, he and I are in full agreement. I sit back and watch as he counts off on his fingers. "The same day you were nearly trampled, someone tried to cut off your hair. Another day a bunch of people tried to kiss you. People literally throw their newborn babies at you. I've already counted six people who've peed their pants in your presence, which, I have to add, is not only upsetting but unsanitary, especially when they try to hug you while they're still wetting themselves." He shakes his head. "The mobs are too big, princess. Too strong. Too passionate. Everyone screams in your face, fights to put their hands on you. And half the time we can't protect you."

"But—"

"I know that most of these people are well intentioned," I say, taking her hand. She turns in her seat, meets my eyes. "They are, for the most part, kind. Curious. Overwhelmed with gratitude and desperate to put a face to their freedom.

"I know this," I say, "because I always check the crowds, searching their energy for anger or violence. And though the vast majority of them are good"—I sigh, shake my head—"sweetheart, you've just made a lot of enemies. These massive, unfiltered crowds are not safe. Not yet. Maybe not ever."

She takes a deep breath, lets it out slowly. "I know you're right," she says quietly. "But somehow it feels wrong not to be able to talk to the people we've been fighting for. I want them to know how I feel. I want them to know much we care—and how much we're still planning on doing to rebuild, to get things right."

"You will," I say. "I'll make sure you have the chance to say all those things. But it's only been two weeks, love. We don't have the necessary infrastructure to make that happen."

"But we're working on it, right?"

"We're working on it," Kenji says. "Which, actually—not that I'm making excuses or anything—but if you hadn't asked me to prioritize the reconstruction committee, I probably wouldn't have issued orders to knock down a series of unsafe buildings, one of which included Winston and Alia's studio, which"—he holds up his hands—"for the record, I didn't know was their studio. And again, not that I'm making excuses for my reprehensible behavior or anything—but how the hell was I supposed to know it was an art studio? It was officially listed in the books as unsafe, marked for demolition—"

"They didn't know it was marked for demolition," Ella says, a hint of impatience in her voice. "They made it into their studio precisely because no one was using it."

"Yes," Kenji says, pointing at her. "Right. But, see, I didn't know that."

"Winston and Alia are your friends," I say unkindly. "Isn't it your business to know things like that?"

"Listen, man, it's been a really hectic two weeks since the world fell apart, okay? I've been busy."

"We've all been busy."

"Okay, enough," Ella says, holding up a hand. She's looking out the window, frowning. "Someone is coming."

Kent.

"What's Adam doing here?" Ella asks. She turns back to look at Kenji. "Did you know he was coming?"

If Kenji responds, I don't hear him. I'm peering out of the very-tinted windows at the scene outside, watching Adam push his way through the crowd toward the car. He appears to be unarmed. He shouts something into the sea of people, but they won't be quieted right away. A few more tries—and they settle down. Thousands of faces turn to stare at him.

I struggle to make out his words.

And then, slowly, he stands back as ten heavily armed men and women approach our car. Their bodies form a barricade between the vehicle and the entrance into the Sanctuary, and Kenji jumps out first, going invisible and leading the way. He projects his power to protect Ella, and I steal his stealth for myself. The three of us—our bodies invisible—move cautiously toward the entrance.

Only once we're on the other side, safely within the boundaries of the Sanctuary, do I finally relax.

A little.

I glance back, the way I always do, at the crowd gathered just beyond the invisible barrier that protects our camp. Some days I just stand here and study their faces, searching for something. Anything. A threat still unknown, unnamed.

"Hey—awesome," Winston says, his unexpected voice shaking me out of my reverie.

I turn to look at him, discovering him sweaty and out of breath.

"So glad you guys are back," he says. "Do any of you happen to know anything about fixing pipes? We've got a kind of sewage problem in one of the tents, and it's all hands on deck."

Our return to reality is swift.

And humbling.

But Ella steps forward, already reaching for the—dear God, is it wet?—wrench in Winston's hand, and I almost can't believe it. I wrap an arm around her waist, tugging her back. "Please, love. Not today. Any other day, maybe. But not today."

"What?" She glances back. "Why not? I'm really good with a wrench. Hey, by the way," she says, turning to the others, "did you know that Ian is secretly good at wood-working?"

Winston laughs.

"It's only been a secret to you, princess," Kenji says.

She frowns. "Well, we were fixing one of the more savable buildings the other day, and he taught me how to use everything in his toolbox. I helped him build a wall," she says, beaming.

"That's a strange justification for spending the hours before your wedding digging feces out of a toilet." Kent again. He's laughing.

My brother.

So strange.

He saunters up to us, a happier, healthier version of him than I've ever seen before. He took a week to recover after we got him back here, but when he regained consciousness and we told him what happened—and assured him that James was safe—he fainted.

And didn't wake up for another two days.

He's become an entirely different person in the days since. Practically jubilant. Happy for everyone. A darkness still clings to all of us—will probably cling to all of us forever—

But Adam seems undeniably changed.

"Just a heads-up," he says, "that we're doing a new thing now. Nouria wants me to go out there and do a general deactivation before anyone enters or exits the grounds. Just as a precaution." He looks at Ella. "Juliette, is that okay with you?"

Juliette.

So many things changed when we came home, and this was one of them. She took back her name. Reclaimed it. She said that by erasing Juliette from her life she feared she was giving the ghost of my father too much power over her. She realized she didn't want to forget her years as Juliette—or to diminish the young woman she was, fighting against all odds to survive. Juliette Ferrars is who she was when she was made known to the world, and she wants it to remain that way.

I'm the only one allowed to call her Ella now.

It's just for us. A tether to our shared history, a nod to our past, to the love I've always felt for her, no matter her name.

I watch her as she laughs with her friends, as she pulls a hammer free from Winston's tool belt and pretends to hit Kenji with it—no doubt for something he deserves. Lily and Nazeera come out of nowhere, Lily carrying a small bundle of a dog she and Ian saved from an abandoned building nearby. Ella drops the hammer with a sudden cry and Adam jumps back in alarm. She takes the filthy beast into her arms, smothering it with kisses even as it barks at her with a wild ferocity. And then she turns to look at me, the animal still yipping in her ear, and I realize there are tears in her eyes. She is crying over a dog.

Juliette Ferrars, one of the most feared, most lauded heroes of our known world, is crying over a dog. Perhaps no one else would understand, but I know that this is the first time she's ever held one. Without hesitation, without fear, without danger of causing an innocent creature any harm. For her, this is true joy.

To the world, she is formidable.

To me?

She is the world.

So when she dumps the creature into my reluctant arms, I hold it steady, uncomplaining when the beast licks my face with the same tongue it used, no doubt, to clean its hindquarters. I remain steady, betraying nothing even when warm drool drips down my neck. I hold still as its grimy feet dig into my coat, nails catching at the wool. I am so still, in fact, that eventually the creature quiets, its anxious limbs settling against my chest. It whines as it stares at me, whines until I finally lift a hand, drag it over its head.

When I hear her laugh, I am happy.

THREE

"Warner?"

"Mr. Warner?"

The invocation of my name in stereo nearly startles me; I absorb this surprise with practiced calm, carefully releasing the dog to the ground. I begin to turn in the direction of the familiar voices, but the liberated creature decides to do nothing with its freedom, instead lifting a paw to my trousers as it whines, yet again, its upturned face imploring me to do something.

Feed it? Pet it?

It barks then, and I spare it a single sharp look, after which it quiets, eyes cast down as its mangy body slumps to the ground, head resting on its paws. The dog settles so close to me its little black snout bumps my boot. I sigh.

"Mr. Warner?" Castle, again.

He and his daughter, Nouria, are staring at me, the latter breaking eye contact only to shoot her father a nearly imperceptible look of frustration.

I glance between them. Clearly, the two still haven't fully settled the specifics of their roles around here.

"Yes?" I say, even as a feeling of unease blooms in my chest.

Castle and Nouria have come to collect me for a private conversation; I can sense this right away. That my mind reaches for anger in response is irrational—I understand this even as it happens—for they cannot know the fear I experience when I leave Ella behind. I have a sudden need to search for her eyes then, to reach for her hand, and I crush the impulse even as my heart rate climbs, a symptom of the new panic lately born in my body. These reactions began shortly after we returned to the Sanctuary; when, to the soundtrack of horrified screams, Ella's limp figure was carted off the plane and planted in the medical tent, where she lived and slept for ten of the fourteen days we've been back. It has been, in a word—*difficult*. And now, whenever I can't see her, my brain tries to convince me she's dead.

Castle says, "Could we steal you for a brief window? Something urgent has come up, and w—"

Nouria presses pause on this statement with a gentle touch to her father's forearm. Her smile is forced.

"I'll need only a few minutes of your time," she says, glancing briefly at someone—Ella, probably—before meeting my eyes again. "I promise it won't take long."

I want to say no.

Instead, I say, "Of course," and finally compel myself to look at Ella, whose steady gaze I have been avoiding. I smile at her as my brain attempts to override its own instincts, to do the calculus necessary to prove my fears a manifestation of an imaginary threat. Every day that Ella remains alive and well is a victory, a concrete set of numbers to add to a column, all of which make it easier for me to do this math; I'm able to process the panic a bit faster now than I did those first few nights. Still—despite my efforts to keep this from her—I have felt Ella watch me. Worry.

Even now, my smile has not convinced her.

She scrutinizes my eyes as she presses a bouquet of newly acquired tools—screwdrivers?—into Kenji's arms. She walks over to me and promptly takes my hand and I'm dealt the blow of an emotional eye roll from our audience. It is a miracle, then, that Ella's love is louder; and I'm so grateful for the reassurance of her touch it pierces me through the chest.

"What's going on?" she says to Nouria. "Maybe I can help."

I catch a note of worry from Nouria then, and, impressive: it never touches her features. She grins when she says, "I think you have enough to do today. Warner and I just have some things we need to discuss. *Privately.*"

She says this last bit in a teasing way, the implication that our discussion might have something to do with the wedding. I stare intently at Nouria, who will not now meet my eyes.

Ella squeezes my hand and I turn to face her.

You okay? she seems to say.

She's done this a lot lately, speaking to me with her thoughts, her emotions.

For a moment, I can only stare at her. A riot of feeling seems to have fused inside me, fear and joy and love

21

and terror now indistinguishable from one another. I lean down, kiss her gently on the cheek. Her skin is so soft I'm tempted to linger, even as the emotional disgust of our audience ratchets only higher.

I've been afraid to touch her lately.

In fact, I've done little more than hold her since we fled Oceania. She nearly died on the flight home. She was already weak when we found Emmaline, having spent most of her energy fighting to kill the poisonous program overriding her mind; worse, she'd torn the tech free from her arm, leaving behind a gaping, gruesome wound. She was still bleeding from her ears, her nose, her eyes, and her teeth when she tore through Max's light, stripping the flesh from her fingers in the process. She was so drained by this point that even with Evie's reinforcements her body was failing. She landed badly and snapped her femur when she fell loose from Max's holding chamber, and then used what little strength she had left to first kill her own sister and then set fire to the capital of Oceania.

When the adrenaline wore off and I saw, for the first time, the edge of severed bone jutting through her pant leg—

The memory is not worth describing.

The next several hours were grim; we had no healers on the flight home, no sufficient pain medication, nothing more than a basic first aid kit. Ella had lost so much blood—and was in such excruciating pain—that she soon fell unconscious. I had no doubt she would die before we touched ground. That she survived that horrific plane ride was its own miracle.

When we finally arrived on base Sonya and Sara did everything they could to help Ella, but they made no promises; even as Ella's physical injuries healed, she was unresponsive. She was incapable of even opening her eyes.

For days, I wasn't sure she would make it.

"Aaron—"

"*Secrets*," I whisper, forcing myself to draw away. "Nothing to worry about."

She studies my eyes. I feel her quietly wage war, happiness and doubt fighting for dominance.

"Good secrets?" she asks hopefully.

My heart lurches at the softness in her voice, the smile that lights up her eyes. I never cease wondering at how skillfully she compartmentalizes her emotions, even in the wake of so much brutality.

Ella is strong where I have forever been weak.

I lost faith in people—in the world—long ago. But no matter how much bloodshed and darkness she experiences, Ella never seems to lose hope in humanity. She is always striving to build a better future. She is always gentle and kind with those she loves.

It is still so strange to me that I am one of those people.

I feel the hum of Castle and Nouria's increasing impatience, and my resentment grows only larger; I generate a fresh smile for Ella and walk away as I do, having left her question unanswered. I don't know what Nouria needs from me, but I fear her news is bleak; no doubt Ella's life is at risk in some new way we'd not anticipated.

The thought alone fills me with dread.

Unbidden, I feel my hands tremble; I shove them in my pockets as I go. The hesitant bark of a mangy dog is soon followed by the sound of its paws tapping the ground, the little beast picking up speed as it hurries to keep pace with me. Briefly, I close my eyes.

This place is a zoo.

Even as I recognize the importance of our work, there remains a regrettably large portion of my mind that finds everyone here detestable—*everything* here detestable.

I am tired.

I want nothing more than to escape this noise with Ella. I want, above all else, for her to be safe. I want people to stop trying to kill her. I want, for the first time in my life, to live in peace, undisturbed; I want to be required by no one but my wife.

These, I realize, are unattainable fantasies.

Castle and Nouria both nod at me as I approach, indicating that I should follow their lead as they turn down the path. I already know they're headed to Nouria and Sam's office—affectionately labeled *the war room*—where we've had many similar meetings.

I glance back just once, hoping to catch a final glimpse of Ella's face, and instead home in on Kenji, whose thoughts are so loud they're impossible to ignore. I experience a flash of anger; I know he's going to follow me even before he moves in my direction.

Between him and the dog trailing me, I'd choose the dog.

Still, both creatures are on my heels now, and I hear Adam laugh as he says something unintelligible to Winston, the two of them no doubt enjoying the spectacle that is my life.

"What?" I say sharply.

The approaching shadow soon evolves into flesh beside me, Kenji matching my strides down the overgrown path, our boots crushing aggressive weeds underfoot. Figures dot the periphery of my vision, their feelings assaulting me as I go. Some of them still think I'm some kind of hero, and are consumed as a result by an idiotic devotion to a warped perception of my identity. My face. My body.

I find these interactions suffocating. Just now, Kenji's anger toward me is so audible I feel it giving me a headache. Still—better anger, I think, than grief.

The collective grief of a crowd is nearly unbearable.

"You know, I really thought you'd be less of an asshole once we got J home," he says flatly. "I see nothing has changed. I see all the efforts I made to defend your shitty behavior were for nothing."

The dog barks. I hear it panting.

It barks again.

"So you're just going to ignore me?" Kenji exhales, irritated. "Why? Why are you like this? Why are you always such a dick?"

Sometimes I'm so desperate for quiet I think I might

commit murder for a moment of silence. Instead, I shut down incrementally, tuning out as many voices as I'm able. It wasn't so bad before I was forced to join this peace cult. In my previous life at Sector 45 I was left alone. At Omega Point, I spent most of my time in solitary confinement. When we later took over 45, I retained the privacy of my rooms.

Here, I am losing my mind.

I am bombarded, en masse, by the emotional downloads of others. There is no reprieve from the pandemonium. Ella likes spending time with these people, and these people do everything in crowds. Meals are taken in a massive dining tent. End-of-day mingling is done communally, in the quiet tent, where it is never quiet. Many of the cabins were damaged or destroyed in the battle, which means everyone is currently sharing space—or sleeping in common areas—while we rebuild. Nouria and Sam did us a kindness by repurposing Ella's room in the medical tent; it seemed the only alternative to bunking with everyone else in a makeshift barracks. Still, our room smells always of antiseptic and death. There is only one narrow hospital bed, over which Ella and I argue each night. She insists, despite my unassailable protests, that I take the bed while she sleeps on the floor.

It's the only time I ever get upset with her.

I don't mind the cold floor. I don't mind physical discomfort. No, what I hate is lying awake every night listening to the pain and grief of others still recovering. I hate being reminded constantly of the ten days I spent standing in the corner of our room watching Ella struggle to come back to life.

My need for silence has grown debilitating. Sometimes I think if I could kill this part of me, I would.

"*Don't touch me,*" I say suddenly, sensing Kenji's intention to make contact with me—to tap my shoulder or grab my arm—before it happens. It takes a great deal of self-control not to physically respond.

"Why do you have to say it like that?" he says, wounded. "Why do you make it sound like I was going to *enjoy* touching you? I'm just trying to get your attention."

"What do you need, Kishimoto?" I ask unkindly. "I'm not interested in your company."

His responding pain is loud; it glances off my chest, leaving a vague impression. This pathetic new development fills me with shame. I desperately don't want to care, and yet—

Ella adores this idiot.

I come to a sudden stop on the path. The dog bumps my legs, wagging its tail violently before barking again. I take a deep breath, stare at a tree in the distance.

"What is it you need?" I ask again, this time gently.

I feel him frown as he processes his feelings. He doesn't look at me when he says, "I just wanted to tell you that I got it."

I stiffen at that, my body activating with awareness. I pivot fully to face him. Suddenly, Kenji Kishimoto appears to me vividly rendered: his tired eyes, his tanned skin, his heavy, sharp black brows—and his hair, in desperate need of a cut. There's a bruise fading along his temple, his left hand wrapped in gauze. I hear the rattle of leaves and spot a squirrel, darting into a bush. The dog goes berserk.

"You got what?" I say carefully.

"Oh, now you're interested?" He meets my eyes, his own narrowed in anger. "Now you're going to look at me like I'm a human being? You know what? Fuck this. I don't even know why I do shit for you."

"You didn't do it for me."

Kenji makes a sound of disbelief, looking away before looking back at me. "Yeah, well, she deserves to have a nice ring, doesn't she? You miserable piece of shit. Who proposes to a girl without a ring?"

"I might remind you that you are in no position to exercise moral superiority," I say, my voice growing lethal even as I will myself to remain calm. "Having *destroyed* her wedding dress."

"That was an accident!" he cries. "Yours was an oversight!"

"Your very existence is an oversight."

"Oh, wow." He throws up his hands. "Ha ha. Very mature comeback."

"Do you have it or not?"

"Yeah. I do." He shoves his hands in his pockets. "But, you know, now I'm thinking I should just give it to her myself. After all, I was the one who did all of this for you. I was the one who asked Winston to sketch your design. I was the one who found someone to make the goddamn thing—"

"*I was not going to leave the grounds while she was lying in a hospital bed*," I say, so close to shouting that Kenji visibly startles. He steps back, studies me a moment.

I neutralize my expression, but too late.

Kenji loses his anger as he stands there, softening as he stares at me. I experience nothing but rage in response.

He never seems to understand. It's his constant pity—his sympathy, not his stupidity—that makes me want to kill him.

I take a step forward, lower my voice. "If you are idiotic enough to think I will allow you to be the one to give her this wedding ring, you have clearly underestimated me. I might not be able to kill you, Kishimoto, but I will devote my life to making yours a palpable, never-ending hellscape."

He cracks a smile. "I'm not going to give her the ring, man. I wouldn't do that. I was just messing with you."

I stare at him. I can hardly speak for wanting to throttle him. "You were just *messing* with me? That was your idea of a joke?"

"Yeah, okay, listen, you are way too intense," he says, making a face. "Juliette would've thought that was funny."

"You clearly don't know her very well if you think so."

"Whatever." Kenji crosses his arms. "I've known her longer than you have, asshole."

At this, I experience an anger so acute I think I might actually kill him. Kenji must see this, because he backpedals.

"No—you're right," he says, pointing at me. "My bad,

29

bro. I forgot about all the memory-wiping stuff. I didn't mean that. I only meant, like— I know her, too, you know?"

"I'm going to give you five seconds to get to your point."

"See? Who says stuff like that?" Kenji's brows furrow; his anger is back. "What does that even mean? What are you going to do to me in five seconds? What if I don't even have a point? No—you know what, I do have a point. My point is that I'm sick of this. I'm sick of your attitude. I'm sick of making excuses for your crappy behavior. I really thought you'd try to be cool for J's sake, especially now, after everything she's been through—"

"I know what she's been through," I say darkly.

"Oh, really?" Kenji says, feigning surprise. "So then maybe you already know this, too"—he makes a dramatic gesture with his hands—"*news flash*: she's, like, a genuinely nice person. She actually gives a shit about other people. She doesn't threaten to murder people all the time. *And she likes my jokes.*"

"She's very charitable, I know."

Kenji exhales angrily and looks around, searching the sky for inspiration. "You know, I've tried, I really have, but I just don't know what she sees in you. She's like—she's like sunshine. And you're a dark, violent rain cloud. Sun and rain don't—"

Kenji cuts himself off, blinking.

I walk away before the realization hits him. Nothing is worth listening to him finish that sentence.

"Oh my God," he says, his voice carrying. "*Oh my God.*"

30

I pick up speed.

"Hey— Don't walk away from me when I'm about to say something awesome—"

"Don't you dare say it—"

"I'm going to say it, man. I have to say it," Kenji says, jumping ahead of me on the path. He's walking backward now, grinning like an idiot.

"I was wrong," he says, making a crude heart shape with his hands. "Sun and rain make a rainbow."

I come to a sudden halt. For a moment, I close my eyes.

"I want to throw up now," Kenji says, still smiling. "Really. Actual vomit. You disgust me."

I'm able to manufacture only mild anger in response to this slew of insults, as the feeling dissipates in the face of irrefutable evidence: Kenji's words belie his emotions. He's genuinely happy for us; I can feel it.

He's happy for Ella, in particular.

I experience a pang at that, at the love and devotion she's inspired in others. It's a rare thing to find even a single person who desires your unqualified joy; she has found many.

She's built her own family.

I exist on the outskirts of this phenomenon: hyperaware that I eclipse her light with my darkness, worried always that she will find me wanting. These relationships mean a great deal to her; I have long known this, and I have tried, for her sake, to be more social. To be nicer to her friends. I don't protest when she asks to gather with the others; I no longer suggest that we take our meals alone together. I follow her around, sitting quietly beside her as she talks and laughs with people whose names I struggle to remember. I watch her bloom in the company of those she cares about, all while I try to drown out their voices, to kill the noise in my head. I worry, constantly, that despite my efforts, I will not be able to be what she wants.

It's true; I am insufferable.

I wonder whether it is only a matter of time before Ella discovers this fact for herself.

Subdued, the fight leaves my body.

"Either give me the ring or leave me alone," I say, hearing the exhaustion in my voice. "Nouria and Castle are waiting for me."

Kenji registers the change in my tone and switches gears, activating in himself a rarely witnessed solemnity. He looks at me for longer than I am comfortable before reaching into his pocket, from which he withdraws a dark blue velvet box.

This, he holds out to me.

I experience an unsettling spike of nerves as I study the box, and collect the object with trepidation, closing my fingers around its soft contours while staring into the distance, trying to collect myself.

I was not expecting to feel like this.

My heart is hammering in my chest. I feel like a nervous child. I wish Kenji were not here to witness this moment, and I wish I cared less about the contents of this box than I actually do, which is impossible.

It's desperately important to me that Ella love it.

Very slowly, I force myself to open the lid, the delicate objects inside catching the light before I've even had a chance to examine them. The rings glitter in the sun, refracting color everywhere. I don't dare remove them from their case, choosing instead only to stare, heart pounding as I do.

I couldn't decide between the two.

Kenji told me it was stupid to get two rings, but as I seldom care for Kenji's opinions, I'd ignored him. Now, as I stare at the set, I wonder if she will think me absurd. One is meant to be an engagement ring, and the other a wedding band—but they are both equally stunning, each in their own way.

The engagement ring is more traditional; the gold band is ultrathin, simple and elegant. There is a single center stone—repurposed from an antique—and though it's quite large, it seemed to me a study in contrasts that reflected how I saw Ella: both powerful and gentle. The jeweler had sent me a selection of stones, each extracted from rings salvaged from different eras. I'd been fascinated by the unusual faceting of an old mine cut diamond. It had been forged by hand a very, very long time ago and was, as a result, slightly imperfect, but I liked that it wasn't machine-made. The tedious, painful honing of a dull but unbreakable stone into a state of dazzling brilliance—it seemed appropriate.

Kenji had assured me there was such a thing as a *princess-cut* diamond, which he thought would be a hilarious choice for Ella, as it recalls his ridiculous nickname for her. I told him I had no interest in choosing a ring based on a joke;

neither did I want my wife's wedding ring reminding her of another man. Besides, when I saw the shape of the stone in question, it felt wrong. The square was too sharp—all hard edges. It didn't remind me of Ella at all.

I asked that the antique stone be placed in a lightly fili-greed, brushed-gold setting, the whisper-thin band of which I wanted to resemble an organic, delicate twig. This design is matched in the wedding band: a fine, curving branch rendered in gold, bare but for two tiny emerald leaves growing on opposite sides of the same path.

"It's really beautiful, man. She's going to love it."

I snap the box shut, returning to the present moment with a disorienting jolt. I look up to discover a contemplative Kenji has been watching me too closely; and I feel so suddenly uncomfortable in his presence that I fantasize, for a moment, about disappearing.

Then, I do.

"*Son of a bitch*," Kenji says angrily. He runs both hands through his hair, glaring at the place I stood. I tuck the velvet box into my pocket and turn down the path.

The dog barks twice.

"That's real mature, bro," Kenji shouts in my direction. "Very nice." Then—acidly—"And *you're welcome*, by the way. Dickhead."

The dog, still barking, haunts me all the way to the war room.

34

FOUR

The unvarnished wooden table has been worn smooth over the years, its raw edges buffed into submission by the calloused hands of rebels and revolutionaries. I run my fingers along the natural grooves, the faded age lines of a long-dead tree. The soft tick of a hanging clock signals what I already know to be true: that I have been here too long, and that every passing second costs me more of my sanity.

"Warner—"

"Absolutely not," I say quietly.

"We've hardly even discussed it. Don't dismiss the idea outright," Nouria says, her flat tone doing little to hide her true frustration, simmering too close to the surface. But then, Nouria is seldom able to hide how much she dislikes me.

I shove away from the table, my chair scraping against wood. It should probably concern me how easily my mind turns to murder for a solution to my problems, but I cannot now dissect these thoughts.

They separated me from Ella for *this*.

"You already know my position on the matter," I say, staring at the exit. "And it's not changing."

"I understand that. I know you're worried about her

35

safety—we're all worried about her safety—but we need help around here. We have to be able to bend the rules a little."

I meet Nouria's eyes then, my own bright with anger. The room shifts out of focus around her and still I see it: dark walls, old maps, a feeble bookshelf stocked with a collection of chipped coffee mugs. The air smells stale. It's depressing in here, shafts of sunlight slicing us all in half.

Things have been far from easy since we took power.

Those who lived well under the reign of The Reestablishment continue to cause us trouble—disobeying missives, refusing to leave their posts, continuing to rule their fiefdoms as if The Reestablishment were still at large. We don't have enough resources quite yet to track all of them down—most of whom know they will be promptly arrested and prosecuted for their crimes—and while some are bold enough to remain at their posts, others have been smart enough to go into hiding, from where they've been hiring mercenaries to carry out all manner of espionage—and inevitably, assassinations. These ex-officials are convening, recruiting ex-supreme soldiers to their side, and attempting to infiltrate our ranks in order to break us from within. They are perhaps the greatest threat to all that we are struggling to become.

I am deeply concerned.

I say little about this to Ella, as she's only just come back to herself in recent days, but our grasp on the world is tenuous at best. History has taught us that revolutions often fail—even after they've won—for fighters and rebels are often unequipped to handle the crushing weight of all they've fought for, and worse: they make for terrible politicians. This is the problem I've always had with Castle, and now with Nouria and Sam.

Revolutionaries are naive.

They don't seem to understand how the world really works, or how difficult it is to sate the whims and wishes of so many. It's a struggle every day to hold on to our lead, and I lose a great deal of sleep thinking about the havoc our enemies will inevitably wreak, the fear and anger they will foment against us.

Still, my own allies refuse to trust me.

"I know we need help," I say coldly. "I'm not blind. But bending the rules means putting Juliette's life at risk. We cannot afford to start bringing in civilians—"

"You won't even let us bring in soldiers!"

"That is patently untrue," I say, bristling. "I never objected to you bringing in extra soldiers to secure the grounds."

"To secure the exterior, yes, but you refused to let us bring them inside the Sanctuary—"

"I didn't *refuse* anything. I'm not the one telling you what to do, Nouria. Lest you forget, those orders came from Juliette—"

"With all due respect, Mr. Warner," Castle interjects, clearing his throat. "We're all aware how much Ms. Ferrars values your opinion. We're hoping you might be able to convince her to change her mind."

I pivot to face him, taking in his graying locs, his weathered brown skin. Castle has aged several years in a short time; these past months have taken their toll on all of us. "You would have me convince her to put her own life at risk? Have you lost your mind?"

"*Hey*," Nouria barks at me. "Watch your tone."

I feel myself stiffen in response; old impulses dare me to reach for my gun. It is a miracle that I am able to speak at all when I say: "Your first offense was separating me from my fiancée on my wedding day. That you would then ask me to allow unvetted persons to enter the only safe space she is allowed in the *entire known world*—"

"They wouldn't be unvetted!" Nouria cries, getting to her feet as she loses her temper. She glows a bit when she's mad, I've noticed, the preternatural light making her dark skin luminous.

"*You* would be there to vet them," she says, gesturing at me from across the table. "You could tell us whether they're safe. That's the whole point of this conversation—to get your cooperation."

"You expect me to follow these people around, then? Twenty-four hours a day? Or did you think it was as simple as making a single deduction and being done with it?"

"It wouldn't be twenty-four hours," she says. "They wouldn't live here—we'd have teams come inside to complete projects, during the day—"

"We've only been in power a matter of weeks. You really

think it wise to start bringing strangers into our inner sanctum? My powers are not infallible. People can hide their true feelings from me," I point out, my voice hardening, "and have done so in the past. I am, therefore, entirely capable of making mistakes, which means you cannot depend on me to be a foolproof defense against unknown entities, which means your plan is faulty."

Nouria sighs. "I will acknowledge that there is a very, very small chance that you might miss something, but I really feel that it might be wor—"

"Absolutely not."

"Mr. Warner." Castle, this time. Softer. "We know this is a lot to ask. We're not trying to put undue pressure on you. Your position here, among us, is critical. None of us know the intricacies of The Reestablishment as well as you do— none of us is as equipped to dismantle, from the inside, the North American system better than you are. We value what you bring to our team, son. We value your opinions. But you have to see that we're running out of options. The situation is dire, and we need your support."

"And this was your plan?" I ask, almost tempted to laugh. "You really thought you could sway me with a bit of good cop, bad cop?" I look at Nouria. "And I take it you're the bad cop?"

"We have more to do than ever before," Nouria says angrily. "We can hardly get our own cabins rebuilt. People need privacy, and proper places to sleep. We need to get the schools running again for the children. We need to stop living off generators and automat dinners." She gesticulates wildly with her arm, accidentally knocking a stack of papers to the floor. "We're struggling to take care of our own people—how can we be expected to take care of the people of 241, or the sectors beyond that?"

She drops her emotional armor for only a second, but I feel it: the weight of her grief is profound.

"We're drowning," she says quietly, running a hand down her face. "We need help. We lost too many of our own in the battle. The Sanctuary is falling apart, and we don't have time to rebuild slowly. The whole world is watching us now. We need more hands on deck, more crews to come in and help us do the work. If we don't, we're going to fail before we've even had a chance to start."

For a moment, I'm silent.

Nouria's not wrong; the Sanctuary is a disaster. So, too, is the planet. I've already sent Haider and Stephan and Lena and the twins back to their respective continents; we needed capable proxies on the ground assessing the current situation abroad—neutralizing chaos wherever possible—and no one was better suited. Nazeera is the only one who stayed behind, claiming that Haider would be fine on his own, that she wanted to stick around for my wedding. I might've been flattered by this nonsense if I didn't know she was lying.

She wanted to stay here to be with Kenji.

Still, I've been grateful for her presence. Nazeera is smart and resourceful and has been an immense help these last couple of weeks. The Sanctuary had enough to do when it was trying only to keep its own people alive; now the entire world is looking to us for direction.

Looking to *Ella* for direction.

What they don't know, of course, is that she's been conscious for only four days. When she finally woke up there was so much for her to do—the world had been waiting for proof that Juliette Ferrars had survived—and despite my many, many protests, she agreed to make limited appearances, to issue statements, to begin discussing what the future might look like for the people. She insisted that we get started right away, that we put together a committee responsible for designing the world's largest public works project—rebuilding towns, schools, hospitals. Investing in infrastructure. Creating jobs, remapping cities.

On a global scale.

Even so, there's hardly been time to think about these things. I spent most of the last two weeks doing what I could to keep Ella alive while trying to put out as many fires as possible. In a moment of honesty I might even be willing to admit that Kenji's mistake—knocking down the wrong building—was almost inevitable. There is an infinite number of things to do and never enough people to do it, or to oversee the details.

Which means we're often making mistakes.

On a micro level, we're also required to pitch in, rebuild our cabins. Cut the grass. Cook the food. Wash the dishes. Ella dragged me into the kitchen as soon as she was able, slapping a pair of questionable rubber gloves against my chest before tugging on a grimy pair of her own, all the while grinning at the gluey bottom of an oatmeal-encrusted cauldron like it was a gift. If Ella were a house, she would be a grand home, one with many rooms and doors, all of which were easily unlocked, flung open.

If I were a house, I would be haunted.

"And I would remind you," Nouria says, her brittle voice returning me to the present, "that you are not the only person on earth ever to have been married. I'm sorry you can't bear to be separated from your fiancée long enough to have a single vital discussion about our failing world, but the rest of us must continue to move, Warner, even if it means deprioritizing your personal happiness."

Her words strike a raw nerve.

"Too true," I say quietly. "There are few, indeed, who've ever prioritized my personal happiness. I wouldn't expect you to be the exception."

I regret the words the moment they've left my mouth.

I steel myself as Nouria reels, processing my uncomfortable moment of honesty. She looks away, guilt flickering, fighting with irritation. Her anger ultimately wins the battle, but when she meets my eyes again, there's a note of regret there, in her gaze, and I realize only then that I have been tricked.

There is more.

I take an imperceptible breath; the true purpose of this meeting is only now about to be revealed to me.

"While we're on the subject," Nouria says, sparing her

father an anxious glance. "I—well. I'm really sorry, Warner, but we're going to have to postpone the wedding."

I stare at her.

My body goes slowly solid, a dull panic working its way through my nervous system. I feel multiple things at once—anger, grief, confusion. A strange sort of resignation rises up above them all, crowning a familiar pain, a familiar fear: that joy, like dew, evaporates from my life the moment I begin to trust the sun.

This is it, then. Par for the course.

"Postpone the wedding," I say, hollow.

"Today is just turning out to be a bad day for everyone," she says, rushing to get the words out. "There's too much going on. There's a major sewage problem we need to get under control, which is using up most of our manpower at the moment, and everyone else is knee-deep in other projects. We don't have enough hands to set up or break things down—and we tried, we really tried to make it work, but we just can't spare the generator tonight. Our electricity has been touch and go, and the temperatures are supposed to be brutal tonight; we can't let the kids freeze in their beds."

"I don't understand. I spoke with Brendan, he offered—"

"Brendan is drained. We've been relying on him too much lately. Winston has already threatened to kill me if we don't let him sleep tonight."

"I see." I stare at the table, then my hands. I have turned to stone, even as my heart races in my chest. "We'd need the generator for only an hour."

"An hour?" Nouria laughs, but she seems unnerved. "Have you ever been to a wedding? Outside? At night? You'd need lights and heat and music. Not to mention all that we'd have to do to get the kitchen going that late, and distributing food— We never got around to making a cake—"

"I don't need a wedding," I say, cutting her off. I sound strange even to myself, nervous. "I just need an officiant. It doesn't have to be a big deal."

"I think it might be a big deal to Juliette."

I look up at that.

I have no worthy response; I can't speak for Ella. I'd never deny her a real wedding if it's what she wants.

The whole thing feels suddenly doomed. The day after I proposed to Ella, she was attacked by her sister, after which she fell into a coma and came home to me nearly dead. We were supposed to have been married this morning, except that her dress was destroyed, and now—

"Postpone until when?"

"I'm not sure, if I'm being honest." Nouria's nerves and apprehension are growing louder now. I try to meet her eyes, but she keeps glancing at Castle, who only shakes his head. "I was hoping maybe we could look at the calendar," she says to me, "think about planning something when things are less crazy around here—"

"You can't be serious."

"Of course I'm serious."

"You know as well as I do," I say angrily, "that there is no guarantee things will ever calm down around here, or

44

that we'll ever be able to get this situation under control—"

"Well, *right now* is a bad time, okay?" She crosses her arms. "It's just a bad time."

I look away. My heart seems to be racing in my head now, pounding against my skull. I feel myself dissociating—detaching from the moment—and struggle to remain present.

"Is this some kind of perverse revenge?" I ask. "Are you trying to prevent my wedding because I won't let you bring in civilians? Because I refuse to put Juliette's life in jeopardy?"

Nouria is quiet for so long I'm forced to look up, to return my mind to itself. She's staring at me with the strangest look in her eyes, something like guilt—or regret—washing her out completely.

"Warner," she says quietly. "It was Juliette's idea."

FIVE

The small velvet box weighs heavy in my pocket, the right angles of which dig into my thigh as I sit here, at the edge of a short cliff, staring down at our very own graveyard. This area was built shortly after the battle—a memorial to all the lives lost.

It's become an unexpected refuge for me.

Few people come through here anymore; for some, the pain is still too fresh, for others, the demands on their time too many. Either way, I'm grateful for the quiet. It was one of the only places to escape while Ella was in recovery, which meant I spent quite a bit of time acquainting myself with this view, and with my seat: a smooth, flat stretch of a massive boulder. The view from this rock is surprisingly peaceful.

Today, it fails to calm me.

I hear a sound then; a distant, faded trill my mind can only describe as birdsong. The dog lifts its head and barks.

I stare at the animal.

The dirty little creature waited for me outside the war room only to follow me here. I've done nothing to inspire its loyalty. I don't know how to get rid of him. Or her.

As if sensing the direction of my thoughts, the dog turns

to face me, panting lightly now, looking for all the world as if it might be smiling. I've hardly had a chance to digest this before it jerks away to bark once more at the sky.

That oddly familiar chirp, again.

I've heard birdsong more often lately; we all have. Castle, who's always insisted all was not lost, claims even now that the animals had not died out entirely. He said that traditionally, birds hide during severe weather, not unlike humans. They seek shelter when experiencing illness, too, during what they believe to be the last moments of their life. He argues that the birds went into mass hiding—either from fear, or from sickness—and that now, with Emmaline's weather manipulations gone, what's left of them have come out of hiding. It's not a foolproof theory, but lately it's grown harder to deny. Even I find myself searching the sky these days, hoping for a glimpse of the impossible creature.

A cold wind barrels through the valley then, pushing through my hair, snapping against my skin. It is with some regret that I realize I left my coat in the war room. The dog whimpers, nudging my leg with its nose. Reluctantly, I rest my hand on what is no doubt its flea-infested head, and the dog quiets. Its thin body curls into a tight ball at my feet, tail tapping the ground.

I sigh.

The day had dawned bright this morning, the sun unencumbered in the sky, but each passing hour has brought with it heavier clouds and an inescapable chill.

Nouria was right; this night will be brutal.

Anxious as I always am to be apart from Ella, my impulses were blunted after meeting with Castle and Nouria. Confused. I wanted nothing more than to seek out Ella; I wanted nothing more than to be alone. I ended up here, in the end—my feet carrying me when my head made no decision—staring into a valley of death, circling the drain of my mind. This morning had been agitating but rewarding; full of irritation but hope, too. I hadn't resented the ticking clock against which I'd been marking time.

In the end, the afternoon has proven empty.

My evening, cleared.

Save the myriad domestic and international disasters that remain unresolved, I've no reason to hurry anymore. I'd thought I was getting married tonight.

As it turns out, I'm not.

I tug free the velvet box from my pocket, clutching it in my fist a moment before taking a sharp breath, then carefully opening the lid. I stare at the glittering contents not unlike a child witnessing fire for the first time. *Naive.*

It's strange: of all the reprehensible things I've known myself to be, I'd never thought I was stupid.

I snap the lid closed, tuck the box back into my pocket.

Nouria didn't lie when she said my wedding wouldn't happen tonight. She didn't lie when she told me it was Ella's idea to postpone. What I don't understand is why Ella never mentioned this to me—or why she said nothing this morning at the dress shop. Perhaps most confusing of all: I've felt no hesitation from her on the matter. Surely, if she didn't want to marry me, I'd have known.

I clench my jaw against the cold.

Somehow, despite the howling wind, the dog appears to have fallen asleep, its body vibrating like a small motor at my feet. I take a moment to study its patchy brown fur, noticing, for the first time, that there's a piece missing from one of its ears.

I exhale, slowly, and rest my elbows on my knees, drop my head into my hands. The small box digs deeper into my flesh.

I'm trying to convince myself to get going—to return to work—when I feel Ella approach. I stiffen, then straighten.

My pulse picks up.

I sense her long before I see her, and when she finally comes into view my heart reacts, contracting in my chest even as my body remains motionless. She lifts a hand when she sees me, the single moment of distraction costing her a fight with a bramble. This area, like so many others, is carpeted in half-dead brush, ripe for a wildfire. Ella struggles to disentangle herself, yanking hard to free her shirt—and promptly frowns when she's released. She studies what appears to be the torn edge of her sweater before looking up at me. She shrugs.

I didn't really care about this sweater anyway, she seems to say, and I can't help but smile.

Ella laughs.

She is windswept. The gusts are growing more aggressive, whipping her hair so that it wraps around her face as she heads in my direction. I can hardly see her eyes; only glimpses of her lips and cheeks, pink with exertion. She swipes at her dark hair with one hand, pushing at overgrown weeds with the other. She is gently rendered in this light, soft in a nondescript sweater the color of moss. Dark jeans. Tennis shoes.

The light changes as she moves, the clouds fighting to hide the sun and occasionally failing. It makes the scene feel dreamlike. She looks so much like herself in this moment that it startles me; it's almost as if she's stepped out of some of my favorite memories.

"I've been looking for you everywhere," she says breathlessly, laughing as she collapses beside me on the boulder. She smells like apricot—it's a new shampoo—and the scent of it fills my head.

She pokes me in the stomach. "Where've you been?"

"Here."

"Very funny," she says, but her smile fades as she studies my face. I find it difficult to meet her gaze.

"Hey," she says softly.

"Hi," I say.

"What's wrong?"

I shake my head slowly. "Nothing."

"Liar," she whispers.

I close my eyes.

I feel myself change when she's near me; the effect is powerful. My body unclenches, my limbs grow heavy. All the tension I carry seems to melt away, taking with it my resolve; I become almost lethargic with relief.

I take a shallow breath.

"Hey," she says again, touching her cool fingers to my face, grazing my cheek. "Who do I have to kill?"

I pull away, smiling faintly at the ground when I say, "Did you tell Nouria you wanted to postpone our wedding?"

Ella's horror is immediate.

She sits back and stares at me, fear and shock and anger coalescing into a single, indistinguishable mass of feeling. I avert my eyes as she processes my question, but her reaction does quite a bit to ameliorate my headspace. Just until she says—

"Yes."

I go unnaturally still.

"But Nouria wasn't supposed to tell you that."

I look up at her then. Ella is trying to hide her panic from me. She looks away, looks into her hands. I don't understand what's happening, and I say this out loud.

Ella can't stop shaking her head. She clasps her hands tight. "Nouria wasn't supposed to tell you that. That wasn't—she wasn't—"

"But it's true."

Ella meets my eyes. "It's technically true, yes, but she shouldn't have— She shouldn't have been the one to say that to you. Nouria and I discussed this a couple of days ago. I'd said that if we couldn't—if we couldn't pull things together in time, that maybe, maybe we could wait—"

"Oh." I squint up into the sky, searching for the sun.

"I was going to tell you myself," she says, more quietly now. "I was just waiting to know . . . more. About how today might turn out. There were some unexpected setbacks this morning, which cost us a lot of time, but I was still hoping we'd be able to figure everything out. Everyone has been working really hard—Kenji told me there was a chance we could still pull it all together today, but if Nouria—"

"I see." I push a hand through my hair, drag it down my neck. "So you discussed this with everyone? Everyone but me."

"Aaron. I'm so sorry. This sounds horrible. I hear it—I hear myself saying it, and I hear how horrible it sounds."

I take a deep, shaky breath. I don't know what to do with my arms, or my legs. They feel prickly suddenly; all pins and needles. I want to tear them off my body.

I'm staring at the ground when I say, "Have you changed your mind? About marrying me?"

"*No*," she says, the word and the emotional force behind it so potent I'm compelled to look up. I see the anguish in her eyes, and I feel it, too; she seems racked with guilt and resignation, an unusual combination of feelings I can't parse. But her love for me is palpable. She takes my hands and the feeling magnifies, flooding my body with a relief so acute I want to lie down.

Something seems to unclench in my chest.

"I love you," she whispers. "I love you so much. I just want to do this right—for both of us. I want you to have a beautiful wedding. I think it matters more to you than you think."

"It doesn't," I say, shaking my head. "I don't care, love. I don't care about any of it. I just want you. I want you to be my family."

She doesn't argue with me. Instead, she squeezes my fingers as her emotions spiral, compound. I close my eyes against the force of it. When I finally look up again, her eyes are shining with unshed tears.

The sight drives a stake into my heart.

"No," I whisper, brushing the backs of my fingers along her jaw, the skin there cold and silken. "Postpone the wedding for as long as you want. We can get married whenever you want, I don't care."

"Aaron—"

I move slowly at first, kissing her cheek and lingering there, pressing my face to the softness of her skin. There's no one here but us. No thoughts but hers and mine. She touches my chest in response, sighing softly as she trails a hand up the back of my neck, into my hair.

My body responds before my mind has had a chance to catch up.

I take her face in my hands and kiss her like I've wanted to for days. *Weeks*. I nudge her mouth open and taste her, running my hands down her body now, drawing her closer.

Her desires consume me as they evolve, leaving me slightly intoxicated. It's always a heady cocktail, experiencing her like this, feeling her emotions in real time. The harder I kiss her the more she wants, the more desperate her needs become. It's dangerous; it makes it hard to think straight, to remember where we are.

She makes a sound when I kiss her neck, a soft moan followed by the whisper of my name, and the combination incites a riot in my body. My hands are under her sweater now, grazing the satin of her skin, the clasp of her bra, and she's reaching for me, for the button of my pants, and I can hear, but choose to ignore, the distant voice in my head telling me that there has to be a better place for this—somewhere warmer, somewhere softer, somewhere that isn't a *graveyard*—

The dog barks loudly, and Ella breaks away from me with a startled cry.

"*Oh my God,*" she says, clutching a hand to her chest. "I didn't— Oh my God. Has the dog been here this whole time?"

I struggle to catch my breath. My heart is pounding in my chest. "Yes," I say, still staring at her.

I pull her back into my arms, claiming her mouth with a single-minded focus that renders the moment surreal, even for me. She's surprised for only a second before she goes soft in my arms, breaking open, kissing me back. I haven't touched her like this in so long—we haven't been together like this in so long—

Something registers in the back of my mind.

I break away, struggling once more to breathe, hoping the muted warning bell in my head was a mistake.

"What's wrong?" Ella says, her hands going to my face. She's still languid with pleasure, her thoughts undiluted by the noise that plagues me always. She kisses my throat, soft and slow. My eyes close.

"Nothing," I whisper, wishing more than ever that we had a bedroom—or even a proper bed. "Nothing. I just thought I heard—"

"Oh my God. *This* is where you guys have been hiding?"

I go suddenly solid, ice chasing away the heat in my veins so fast I almost shudder.

"*Crap,*" Ella whispers.

"You two have no shame, huh? You were just going to desecrate a graveyard? Can't even keep your clothes on in this freezing weather?"

"Kenji," Ella says quietly. The word is a warning.

"What?" He crosses his arms. "I've said it before and I'll say it again: *gross.* I think I need to go bleach my eyes."

I help Ella to her feet, drawing an arm around her waist. "What do you want?" I say to Kenji, entirely unable to rein in my anger.

"Nothing from you, buddy, thanks. I'm here because I need Juliette."

"Why?" Ella and I ask at the same time.

Kenji blows out a breath, looking away once before looking back at Ella. Cryptically, he says, "I just need you to come with me, okay?"

"Oh." Her eyes widen a fraction. "Okay."

"What's wrong?" I ask. "Do you need help?"

Ella shakes her head. I feel her apprehension, but she pastes on a smile. "No, it's nothing—just boring stuff out on unregulated turf. We actually managed to track down one of the pre-Reestablishment city planners in this area, and he's coming by to discuss our ideas."

"Oh," I say.

Ella is hiding something.

I can feel it—can feel that she's not being entirely truthful. The realization provokes a sinking feeling in my gut that scares me.

"You won't miss me, right?" Her smile is strained. "I know you always have a ton of stuff to do."

"Yes." I look away. "There's always a great deal to accomplish."

A pause. "So—I'll see you tonight?"

"Tonight?" I glance at Ella, then the sun.

There are still hours left before nightfall, which means she intends to be gone for all of them. My mind is overrun with doubt. First our wedding, now this. I don't understand why Ella isn't being honest with me. I want to say something to her, to ask her a direct question, but not here, not in front of Kenji—

Ella's emotions take a sudden turn.

I look up to find her staring at me now with concern, with a palpable fear—for *me*.

"Or I can stay here," she says more quietly. "I don't have to go anywhere."

"Uh, yes, princess, you do—"

"Be quiet, Kenji."

"We need you out there," he insists, throwing his arms

wide. "You have to be there—we can't just deci—"

"Aaron," Ella says, placing a hand on my chest. "Are you going to be okay?"

I stiffen, then step back.

The question inspires in me a reaction I do not admire. I bristle at the sympathy in her voice, at the thought that she might think me incapable of surviving a few hours on my own.

Understanding hits me with the force of a sledgehammer: Ella thinks I am broken.

"I'll be fine," I say, unable to meet her eyes. "I have, as you said, a great deal to do."

"Oh," she says carefully. "Okay."

I can still feel her studying me, and though I don't know what she sees in my face, my expression appears to have convinced her that I won't turn to dust in her absence. An approximation of the truth.

A tense silence stretches out between us.

"All right, great," Ella finally says, all false brightness. "So, I'll see you tonight? Or sooner— I mean, depending on how quickly I can—"

Kenji makes a sound; something like a choked laugh. "Yeah, if I were you, I'd clear my schedule."

"Love," I say quietly. "Are you sure everything is okay?"

"Absolutely," she says, straining to smile wider. She squeezes my hand, kissing me briefly before pulling away. "I promise. I'll be back as soon as I can."

Ella is still lying. It hits me like a blow.

"Hey, sorry about the wedding, man," Kenji says, making a face. "Who knew the downside of overthrowing a corrupt government was that we'd have absolutely no free time?"

I swallow, hard, ignoring the fresh vise around my chest. "I see everyone already knows about that."

"Yeah, I mean, it was J's idea to postpone. There's just so much to do, and trying to have the wedding at night was going to be really complicated, and she thought it would be better to jus—"

"*Kenji*," she says sharply. She shoots him a look I can't entirely decipher, but her anger surprises me.

"My bad, princess." Kenji holds up both hands. "My bad. I didn't realize it was controversial to let the groom know what was happening with his own wedding, but I guess I just don't know how weddings work, do I?" He says that last part with an edge, irritation souring his expression.

I have no idea what's going on between them.

Ella rolls her eyes, more frustrated with Kenji than I've ever seen her. She practically stomps toward him, hugging herself against the cold. I hear her mutter, "You're going to pay for that," before they're off, the two of them disappearing into the distance without a backward glance.

Without me.

I stand there for so long after they're gone that the sun finally moves toward the horizon, taking with it any lingering warmth. I shiver slightly as the temperatures plummet, but I can ignore the cold. I cannot, however, seem to ignore the dull ache in my chest.

When I woke up this morning I'd thought this would be the happiest day of my life. Instead, as the day approaches dusk—

I feel hollow.

The dog barks suddenly, a series of sharp yaps in a row. When I turn to face the creature it makes an altogether different sound, something like a growl, and jumps up enthusiastically, lifting its paws to my pant leg. I give the animal a firm look, indicating with my index finger that it should disengage immediately. It sinks, slowly, back onto its feet, tail wagging.

Another bark.

I sigh at the sight of its eager, upturned face. "I suppose I shouldn't be ungrateful. You seem to be the only one interested in my company today."

A bark.

"Very well. You may come with me."

The dog rises up onto all four legs, panting, tail wagging harder.

"But if you defecate on any interior surface—or chew up my boots, or urinate on my clothes—I will put you right back outside. You will hold your bowel movements until you are a considerable distance away from me. Is that clear?"

Another responding bark.

"Good," I say, and walk away.

The dog chases after me so quickly its snout bumps my heels. I listen to the sound of its paws hitting the ground; I can hear it breathing, sniffing the earth.

"First," I tell it, "someone needs to give you a bath. Not me, obviously. But someone."

The dog gives an aggressive, eager yap at that, and I realize with a start that I'm able to get a bead on its emotions. The reading, however, is imprecise; the creature doesn't always understand what I'm saying, so its emotional responses are inconsistent. But I see now that the dog understands essential truths.

For some inexplicable reason, this animal trusts me. More perplexing: my earlier declaration made it happy.

I don't know much about dogs, but I've never heard of one that enjoyed being bathed. Though it occurs to me then that if the animal understood the word *bath*, it must once have had an owner.

I come to a sudden stop, turning to study the creature: its matted brown fur, its half-eaten ear. It pauses when I do, lifting a leg to scratch behind its head in an undignified manner.

I see now that it's a boy.

Otherwise, I have no idea what kind of dog this is; I wouldn't even know how to begin classifying his species. He's obviously some kind of mutt, and he's either young, or naturally small. He has no collar. He's clearly underfed. And yet, a single glance at its nether regions confirmed that the animal had been neutered. He must've once had a proper home. A family. Though he likely lost his owner some time ago to have been reduced to this half-feral state.

I'm compelled to wonder, then, what happened.

I meet the dog's deep, dark eyes. We're both quiet, assessing each other. "You mean to tell me that you *like* the idea of taking a bath?"

Another happy bark.

"How strange," I say, turning once more down the path. "So do I."

SIX

By the time I step foot in the dining tent, it's already nine o'clock. Ella has been gone several hours now, and I have succeeded only a little in distracting myself from this fact. I know, intellectually, that she is not in danger; but then, my mind has always been my fiercest adversary. All the day's compounding uncertainties have led to a mounting apprehension in my body, the experience of which recalls the sensation of sandpaper against my skin.

The worst uncertainties are the ones I cannot kill or control.

In the absence of action I am forced instead to marinate in these thoughts, the anxiety abrading me more in every minute, corroding my nerves. So thorough is this excoriation that my entire body is rendered an open wound in the aftermath, so raw that even a metaphorical breeze feels like an attack. The mental exertion necessary to withstand these simple blows leaves me worse than irritable, and quick to anger. More than anything, these exhausting efforts make me want to be alone.

I don't know what's happening anymore.

I scan the dining tent as I head toward the unusually short serving line, searching for familiar faces. The interior space isn't nearly as large as it once was; a great portion of it has been sectioned off to use for temporary sleeping arrangements. Still, the room is emptier than I expect. There are only a few people occupying the scattered dining tables, none of whom I know personally—save one.

Sam.

She's sitting alone with a stack of papers and a mug of coffee, fully absorbed in her reading.

I make my way through the tables to stand in the short serving line, accepting, after a brief wait, my foil bowl of food. I choose a seat for myself in a far corner of the room, sitting down with some reluctance. I waited as long as I could to have this meal with Ella, and eating alone feels a bit like admitting defeat. It is perhaps maudlin to ruminate on this fact, to imagine myself abandoned. Still, it's how I feel.

Even the dog is gone.

It disturbs me to I think I might trade the relative quiet of this room for its regular chaos if only to have Ella by my side. It's an unnerving thought, one that does nothing but magnify my childish longing.

I tear back the foil lid and stare at its contents: a single gelatinous mass of something resembling stir-fry. I set my plastic fork on the table, sit back in my seat. Nouria was right about one thing, at least.

This is unsustainable.

After finding someone to take the dog, I spent the afternoon catching up on digital correspondence, most of which required fielding calls and perusing reports from the supreme kids, all of whom are dealing with different—and equally concerning—dilemmas. Luckily, Nazeera helped us set up a more sophisticated network here at the Sanctuary, which has since made it easier to be in touch with our international counterparts. The Sanctuary has been great for many things, but there has been, since the beginning, a dearth of accessible technology. Omega Point, by comparison, was home to formidable, futuristic tech that was impressive even by The Reestablishment's standards. This quality of tech, I realized, was something I'd taken for granted; as it turns out, not all rebel headquarters are built equally.

When I realized the Sanctuary was to be our new, permanent home, I insisted we make changes. This was when Nouria and I first discovered the depth of our mutual dislike.

Unlike Sam, Nouria is quick to wound; she is injured too easily by perceived slights against her camp—and her leadership—which has made it difficult to push for change. Progress.

Still, I pushed.

We took as much hardware from the local military headquarters as we were able, sacrificing what was once the elementary school tent to piece together a functioning command center, the capabilities of which were entirely unfamiliar to both Nouria and Sam, who still refuse to learn more than its most basic functions.

Lucky for them, I don't need assistance.

I do my work most days surrounded by the ancient

hieroglyphics of sticky children; crayon drawings of inde-cipherable creatures are thumbtacked to the wall above my desk; crudely formed bees and butterflies flutter from the ceiling. I hang my jacket on a rack painted in colors of the rainbow, slinging my gun holster around the back of a small yellow chair decorated with handprints.

The disturbing dichotomy is not lost on me.

Still, between Nazeera and Castle—who surprised me by revealing he was the mastermind behind most of Omega Point's innovative tech—we're close to designing an inter-face that would rival what we'd built at Sector 45.

I buried myself in work for hours, hardly coming up for air, not even to eat. In addition to all else, I've been designing a plan—a safer plan—that would help us bring in the assis-tance we need while mitigating our risk of exposure. Ella's, most of all. Usually, this kind of work is enough to hold my focus. But today, of all days—a day my mind continues to remind me was meant to be my wedding day—

It doesn't matter what I do; I am distracted.

I sigh, resting my hands on my thighs, too uncomfort-ably aware of the little velvet box still tucked into my pocket.

I clench, unclench my fists.

I scan the dining room again, restless with nervous energy. It's still surprising to me how easily I shed my solitude for the privilege of Ella's company. The truth is, I learned to enjoy the mechanics of life with her by my side; her presence renders my world brighter, the details richer. It is impossible not to feel the difference when she is gone.

Still, this has been a strange and difficult day.

I know Ella loves me—and I know she means it when she says she wants to be with me—but today has been ripe not merely with disappointment but also concerning obfuscations. Ella is hiding something from me, and I have been waiting all day for her to return so that I might ask her, privately, a single clarifying question that might resolve this incertitude. Until then, it's hard to know how to feel, or what to believe.

More simply: I miss her.

I regret even relinquishing the dog.

Upon my return from the gravesite, I searched the grounds for a familiar face—to find someone to take him—and despite my efforts, I couldn't find anyone I recognized. There's a great deal of work to do in the previously unregulated areas outside the Sanctuary, so it's not surprising to see people gone; I was only surprised to find myself disappointed. All I've wanted for so long was a single moment of quiet, and now that I have it in abundance, I'm not sure I want it.

The realization has quietly shocked me.

Regardless, I was about to abandon the idea of bathing the animal when a nervous young woman approached me, her face as red as her hair as she stammered aloud a suspicion that I might need help.

I appreciated the effort on her part, but the conversation was far from ideal.

The girl turned out to be a part of a persistent, ridiculous subsection of people here at the Sanctuary, a lingering group of men and women who still insist on treating me like I'm some kind of a hero. I fought off my father's supreme soldiers in a failed attempt at protecting Ella, and these well-meaning fools have somehow idealized this failure; one of the worst days of my life now fossilized in their memories as a day that should be celebrated.

It makes me ill.

They've romanticized me in their minds, these people, romanticized the very idea of my existence, and often objectify me in the process. Every time I looked this young woman in the eye she would visibly tremble, her feelings both indecent and sincere, the mixture of which was almost too uncomfortable to recount.

I thought she might be more at ease if I stared at the animal as I spoke, which I did, and which seemed to calm her. I told her about the dog—explaining that he needed a bath, and food—and which she generously offered to take into her care. As I sensed no actual danger from the girl, I accepted her overture.

"Does he have a name?" she'd asked.

"He is a dog," I'd said, frowning as I looked up. "You may call him a dog."

The young woman froze at that, at our sudden eye contact. I watched her pupils dilate as she grappled with an emotional combination too often flung in my direction: abject terror and desire. It confirmed for me then what I've always known to be true—that most people are disappointing and should be avoided.

She said nothing to me after that, only scooping up the reluctant, whining animal into her trembling arms and shuffling away. I've not seen either of them since.

It would not be an exaggeration to say that this day has been a thorough disappointment.

I push back my chair and get to my feet, taking the foil bowl to go; I plan to save the food-adjacent mass for the dog, should I ever see him again. I glance up at the large clock on the wall, noting that I managed only to kill another thirty minutes.

Quietly, I acknowledge I should accept this day for the nonevent it turned out to be—and, as it appears unlikely I will see Ella tonight, I should go to bed. Still, I'm demoralized by this turn of events; so much so that it takes me a moment to realize Sam is calling my name.

I pivot in her direction.

She's waving me over, but I have no interest in a conversation right now. I want nothing more than to retreat, fester in my wounds. Instead, I force myself to clear the short distance between us, unable to generate even a modicum of warmth as I approach.

I stare at her by way of hello.

Sam is even more exhausted than I first assumed, her eyes held up by lavender half-moons. Her skin is grayer than I've ever seen it, her short blond hair limp, falling into her face.

She spares no time for formalities, either.

"Have you read the recent incident reports from"—she looks down at her papers, rubbing one eye with the palm of her hand—"18, 22, 36, 37, 142 through 223, and 305?"

"Yes."

"Have you noticed what they all have in common?"

I sigh, feeling my body tense anew when I say, "Yes."

Sam folds her arms atop her stack of papers, peering up at me from her seat. "Great. Then you'll understand why we need Juliette to tour the continent. She has to make appearances—physical appearances—"

"No."

"They are rioting in the streets, Warner." Sam's voice is unusually hard. "Against *us*. Not against The Reestablishment—against *us*!"

"People are impatient and ungrateful," I say sharply. "Worse: they are stupid. They don't understand that change takes time. Clearly they assumed that the fall of The Reestablishment would bring instant peace and prosperity to the world, and in the two weeks since we've been in power, they can't understand why their lives haven't miraculously improved."

"Yes, okay, but the solution isn't in ignoring them. These people need hope—they need to see her face—"

"She's done televised broadcasts. She's made a couple of local appearances—"

"*It's not enough*," Sam says, cutting me off. "Listen. We all know the only reason Juliette isn't doing more is because of you. You're so worried about keeping *her* safe that you're putting our entire movement in jeopardy. She did this, Warner. It was her choice to take on The Reestablishment—it was her choice to carry this burden. The world needs her now, which means you have to get your shit together. You have to be braver than this."

I stiffen at that, at the surgical precision of her blade.

I say nothing.

Sam exhales in the wake of my silence, something like a laugh. "You think I don't understand what it's like to be with someone whose life is constantly in danger? You think I don't understand how terrifying it is to watch them step foot out the door every day? Do you have any idea how many attempts have been made on Nouria's life?"

Still, I say nothing.

"It's really fucking hard," she says angrily, surprising me with her language. Sam pushes both hands through her hair before rubbing her eyes again. "It's really, really, *really* hard."

"Yes," I say quietly.

She meets my eyes then. "Look. I know you're not doing this on purpose. I know you only want the best for her. But you're holding her back. You're holding all of us back. I don't know exactly what you two have been through—whatever it was, it must've been serious, because Juliette's clearly more worried for you than she is for herself, but—"

"What?" I frown. "That's not—"

"Trust me. She and I have had a lot of conversations about this. Juliette doesn't want to do anything to scare you. She thinks you're processing something right now—she wouldn't tell me what—and she's adamant that she won't do anything risky until she's sure you can handle it. Which means I need you to handle it. Now."

"I'm doing *fine*," I say, my jaw clenching.

"Wonderful." Sam generates a smile. "If you're doing fine, go ahead and tell her that. Encourage Juliette to go on an international tour—or at minimum, a national one. Juliette knows how to talk to crowds; when she's looking people in the eye they *believe* her. I know you've seen it. In fact, you probably know better than anyone that no one cares more about these people than she does. She genuinely cares about their families, their futures—and right now, the world needs a reminder. They need reassurance. Which means you have to let her do her job."

I feel my heart rate spike. "I would never keep her from doing her job. I just want her to be safe."

"Yes—you prioritize her safety above all else, to the detriment of the world. You're making decisions from a place of fear, Warner. You can't help heal the planet if you're only thinking about what's best for one person—"

"I never got into this to heal the planet," I say sharply. "I have never pretended to care about the future of our pathetic civilization, and if you ever took me for a revolutionary, that was your mistake. I see now that I have to make something clear, so remember this: I would happily watch the world go up in flames if anything happened to her, and if that's not enough for you, you can go to hell."

Sam shoves back her chair so fast it makes a piercing, skin-crawling screech that echoes around the near-empty dining tent. She's on her feet now, boring a hole in the floor

71

with the heat of her anger. The few faces still dotting the room turn to look at us; I feel their surprise, their mounting curiosity. Sam is diminutive in stature, but fierce when she chooses to be, and right now she looks as if she's considering killing me with her bare hands.

"You are not special," she says. "You are not the only one of us who's ever suffered. You're not the only one who lies awake at night worrying for the safety of their loved ones. I have no sympathy for your pain, or your problems."

"Good," I say, more than matching her anger. "As long as we understand each other."

Sam shakes her head and throws up her hands, looking for a moment like she might laugh. Or cry. "What on earth does she see in you? You're nothing but a callous, cold-hearted narcissist. You don't care about anyone but yourself. I hope you know how lucky you are that Juliette tolerates your presence. You wouldn't even be here if it weren't for her. I sure as hell wouldn't vouch for you."

I lower my eyes, absorbing these blows with studied indifference. My body is not unlike the moon, cratered so thoroughly by brutality it's hard to imagine it untouched by violence.

"Good night," I say quietly, and turn to leave.

I hear Sam sigh, her regret building as I walk away. "Warner, wait," she says, calling after me. "I'm sorry—that was over the line— It's been a long day, I didn't mean—"

I don't look back.

SEVEN

I'm sandwiched between two thin blankets on the frozen floor of this hospital room, eyes closed, pretending to sleep, when I hear the soft whine of the door, Ella's familiar presence entering the room.

It's hours past midnight.

She brings with her the faint smell of something slightly chemical, which confuses me, but more important: I feel her fear as she tiptoes into the space, all displaced by a sudden relief when she catches sight, no doubt, of my prone body.

Relief.

I don't understand.

She is relieved to discover me asleep. She is relieved she doesn't have to speak with me.

The pressure in my chest intensifies.

I listen to the sounds of her shedding her shoes and clothes in the dark, wondering how best I might shatter the silence, bracing myself for her surprise—then disappointment—to discover I am awake. I give her a moment, hearing the familiar sounds of sheets rustling. I'm imagining her climbing into the narrow hospital bed, tucking herself under the covers, when her emotions pivot without warning: she experiences a sharp, stunning wave of happiness.

Somehow, this only scares me more.

Ella is not merely relieved, then, but *happy* to have evaded me. She's happy to be going to sleep without being disturbed.

My heart races faster, dread multiplying. I'm almost afraid to say anything now, knowing that the sound of my voice would only prompt the demolition of her joy. Still, I have to speak with her. I need to know what's happening between us—and I'm preparing to say as much when I hear her breathing change.

She is already asleep.

I have been lying awake fully clothed, sinking into darkness for hours. Ella has fallen asleep in moments.

I feel frozen. Fastened to this cold floor by fear, familiar pins and needles sparking to life in my limbs.

My eyes fly open; I can't seem to breathe.

I hadn't known what to do with the jewelry box in my pocket. I was afraid to leave it somewhere, worried it might be misplaced, or discovered. It remains with me instead, branding my leg with its presence, reminding me of all that feels suddenly and terrifyingly lost.

Unconsciously, I reach for an altogether different piece of jewelry, my fingers finding the smooth stone of the jade ring in the dark, the piece so much a part of me now that I can't remember what my hand looks like without it. I spin the cold band around my pinkie finger in a familiar, repetitive motion, wondering whether it has been a mistake, all these years, to keep this token of grief so close to my skin.

The ring had been a gift from my mother; it was the only present I'd ever received as a child. And yet, the memories associated with this object are so dark and painful—reminders in every moment of my father's tyranny, my mother's suffering, my grandfather's betrayal—

I have often wanted to lock away this memento of my tortured childhood. Touching it even now reminds me of versions of myself—six years old, then seven, eight, nine, and on and on—that once clutched it desperately even as I screamed, explosive pain branching across my back, over and over.

For a long time, I hadn't wanted to forget. The ring reminded me always of my father's brutality, of the hatred that motivated me to stay alive if only to spite him.

More than that, it is all I have left of my mother.

And yet, perhaps this ring has tethered me to my own darkness, this symbol of infinite repetition fated to conjure, forever, the agonies of my past.

Sometimes I fear I will be trapped forever in this cycle: incapable of happiness, inseparable from my demons.

I close my eyes, scenes from the day replaying as if on an automatic loop. I seem doomed to relive the events in perpetuity, combing them for answers, for evidence of anything that might explain what's happening to my life. And despite my best efforts to shut them out, I recall Sam's voice, then Kenji's—

You're nothing but a callous, coldhearted narcissist.

I hope you know how lucky you are that Juliette tolerates your presence.

I'm sick of your attitude.

I'm sick of making excuses for your crappy behavior.

I just don't know what she sees in you.

What on earth does she see in you?

EIGHT

When I open my eyes, the light is filtering through the half-closed curtains, blinding me. I can tell just by its position in the room that the sun is new; the morning is young.

I don't know when I fell asleep; I don't even know how I managed to accomplish this feat except through sheer exhaustion. My body succumbed to the need even as my mind refused, protesting this decision with a series of nightmares that begin to replay as I sit up, closing my eyes against the glare.

I spent the night outrunning an indecipherable natural disaster. It was that vintage of vague dream-element that makes sense only in the dream and none at all upon waking.

I couldn't stop running.

I had no choice but to keep moving for fear of being decimated by the impending calamity, searching all the while for Ella, from whom I had been separated. When I finally heard her voice it was from high above: Ella was sitting in a tree, far from danger, staring happily at the clouds as I ran for my life. The disaster—something like a tornado or tsunami or both—increased in intensity, and I picked up speed, unable to slow down long enough to speak with her, or even to climb the tree, whose trunk was so impossibly tall I couldn't understand how she'd scaled it.

In a desperate effort I called her name, but she didn't hear me; she was turned away, laughing, and I realized then that Kenji was sitting in the tree with her. So was Nazeera, who'd no doubt flew them both to safety.

I screamed Ella's name once more, and this time she turned at the sound of my voice, meeting my eyes with a kind smile. I finally stopped then, falling to my knees from overexertion.

Ella waved at me just as I was pulled under.

A sharp knock at the hospital door has me upright in a moment, my mind on a delay even as my instincts sharpen. I notice only then that Ella is not here. Her rumpled hospital sheets are the only evidence she ever was.

I drag a hand down my face as I head for the door, faintly aware that I'm still in the clothes I was wearing yesterday. My eyes are dry, my stomach empty, my body exhausted.

I am wrung out.

I open the door, so surprised to see Winston's face that I take a step back. I seldom—if ever—speak with Winston. I've never had any specific reason to dislike him, but then, he and I are ill-acquainted. I don't even know if I've ever seen his face from so close a distance.

"Wow," he says, blinking at me. "You look like shit."

"Good morning."

"Right. Yeah. Good morning." He takes a deep breath

and attempts a smile, adjusting his black glasses for no reason but nerves.

Winston, I'm baffled to discover, is *very* nervous to be
near me.

"Sorry, I was just surprised," he says, rushing his words.
"You're usually really—you know, like, put together. Anyway you might want to take a shower before we get going."

I'm so unable to process the absurdity—or the audacity—
of this request, that I close the door in his face. Turn the
lock.

The pounding begins immediately after. "Hey," he says,
shouting to be heard. "I'm serious— I'm supposed to take
you to breakfast this morning, but I really th—"

"I don't need a chaperone," I say, pulling off my sweater.
This hospital room is one of the larger ones, with an en
suite, industrial bathroom/shower combination. "And I
don't need you to remind me to bathe."

"I didn't mean it as an insult! Damn." A nervous laugh.
"Literally everyone tried to warn me that you were hard to
deal with, but I thought maybe they were exaggerating, at
least a little. That was my mistake. Listen, you look fine.
You don't smell or anything. I just think you'll want to take
a shower—"

"Again, I don't need your advice on this matter." I'm
stepping out of my pants, folding them carefully to contain
the small box still trapped in the pocket. "Leave."

I turn on the shower, the sound of which distorts

79

Winston's voice. "Come on, man, don't make this difficult. I was the only one willing to come get you this morning. Everyone else was too afraid. Even Kenji said he was too tired today to deal with your shit."

I hesitate then.

I abandon the bathroom, returning to the closed door in only my boxer briefs. "Come get me for what?"

I feel Winston startle at the sound of my voice, so close. He equivocates, saying only: "Um, yeah, I can't actually tell you."

A terrifying unease moves through me at that. Winston's guilt and fear is palpable, his anxiety growing.

Something is wrong.

I glance one last time at Ella's empty bed before unlatching the lock. I'm only dimly aware of my appearance, that I'm opening the door in my underwear. I'm reminded swiftly of this fact when Winston does an exaggerated double take upon seeing me.

He quickly averts his eyes.

"Fucking hell—why did you have to take off your clothes?"

"What is going on?" I ask coldly. "Where is Juliette?"

"What? I don't know." Winston is turned away entirely now, pinching the bridge of his nose between his thumb and index finger. "And I'm not allowed to tell you what's going on."

"Why not?"

He looks up at that, meeting my eyes for only a nano-second before turning sharply away; a mottled heat rushes up his neck, burns his ears. "Please, for the love of God," he says, yanking off his glasses to rub at his face. "Put on some clothes. I can't talk to you like this."

"Then leave."

Winston only shakes his head, crossing his arms against his chest. "I can't. And I can't tell you what's going on, because it's supposed to be a surprise."

The fight leaves my body in a single gust, leaving me light-headed. "A surprise?"

"Can you please go take a shower? I'll wait for you outside the MT. Just—just show up with your clothes on. *Please.*"

I let the door slam shut between us, then stare at it, my heart pounding wildly in my chest. There's a wave of relief from Winston, then a flicker of happiness.

He seems—excited.

I finally walk away, stepping out of my underwear and tossing it into a nearby laundry bin before entering the quickly steaming bathroom. I catch my reflection in the floor-length mirror affixed to the wall, my face and body being devoured slowly by steam.

It's supposed to be a surprise.

For a protracted moment, I can't seem to move. My eyes, I notice, are dilated in this dim light—darker. I look slightly different to myself, my body hardening by degrees every day.

I've always been toned, but this is different. My face has lost any lingering softness. My chest is broader, my legs more firmly planted. These slight changes in muscle definition, in vascularity—

I can see myself getting older.

Our research for The Reestablishment indicated that there was once a time when the *twenties* were considered the prime years of youth. I always struggled to visualize this world, one wherein teenagers were treated like children, where those in their twenties felt young and carefree, their futures boundless.

It sounded like fiction.

And yet—I have often played this game in the privacy of my mind. *In another world, I might live in a house with my parents.* In another world, I might not even be expected to have a job. In another world, I might not know the weight of death, might never have held a gun, shot a bullet, killed so many. The thoughts register as absurd even as I think them: that in an alternate universe I might be considered some kind of adolescent, free from responsibility.

Strange.

Was there ever truly a world wherein parents did the job expected of them? Was there ever a reality in which the adults were not murdered merely for resisting fascism, leaving their young children behind to raise themselves?

Here, we are nearly all of us a contingent of orphans roaming—then running—this broken planet.

I often imagine what it would be like to step into such an

alternate reality. I wonder what it would be like to set down the weight of darkness in exchange for a family, a home, a refuge.

I abandon my reflection to step under the hot water.

I never thought I'd come close to touching such a dream; I never thought I'd be able to trust, or love, or find peace. I've been searching for so long for a pocket of quiet to inhabit, a place to exist unencumbered. I always wanted a door I might close—for even a moment—against the violence of the world. I didn't understand then that a home is not always a place. Sometimes, it's a person.

I would sleep on the cold floor of our hospital room for the rest of my life if it meant staying by Ella's side. I can forgo quiet. I can compartmentalize my need for space. My desire for privacy.

But to lose *her*—

I close my eyes against the water pressure, the jet forging tributaries against my face, my body. The heat is a balm, welcome against my skin. I want to burn off the residue of yesterday. I want an explanation for all that happened—or even to forget it altogether. When things are out of alignment between myself and Ella, I can't focus. The world seems colorless; my bones too large for my body. All I want, more than anything else, is to bridge the distance between us.

I want this uncertainty gone.

I turn my face up toward the jet, closing my eyes as the water pelts my face. I breathe deep, drawing in water and steam, trying to steady my heartbeat.

I know better than to be optimistic, but even as I forbid myself to think it, I cannot help but reflect that the word *surprise* is seldom associated with something negative.

It might've been a poor choice of words on Winston's part, but his moment of excitement seemed to confirm this choice; he might've chosen a more pejorative term had he wished to manage my expectations of disappointment.

Despite my every silent protest, hope takes hold of me, forces from me the dregs of my composure. I lean my forehead against the cool tile, the water beating the scars on my back. I can hardly feel it, the sensations there dulled from nerve damage. Scar tissue.

I straighten at a sudden sound.

I turn, heart racing, at the soft shudder of the bathroom door opening. I already know it's her. I always feel her before I can see her, and when I see her—when she opens the bathroom door and stands there, smiling at me—

My relief is so acute I reach for the wall, bracing myself against the cold tile. Ella is holding two mugs of coffee, dressed the way she often is: in a soft sweater and jeans, her dark brown hair so long now it skims her elbows. She grins at me, then disappears into the outer room, and I start to follow her, nearly slipping in my haste. I catch the doorframe to steady myself, watching as she rests the coffee mugs on a nearby table. She slips off her tennis shoes. Tugs off her socks.

When she pulls her sweater over her head, I have a minor heart attack. She's facing away from me, but her back is bare. She's not wearing a bra.

"You were sound asleep this morning," she says, glancing over her shoulder at me as she unbuttons her jeans. "I was afraid to wake you up. I went out to get us some coffee, but the line at breakfast was really long. I'm sorry I wasn't here."

She shimmies out of her jeans then, tugging them down over her hips. She's wearing a scrap of lace masquerading as underwear, and I watch, immobilized, as she bends over to yank off the last of the jeans, pulling her feet free.

When she turns around, I'm struggling to breathe.

She's so beautiful I can hardly look at her; I feel as if I've stepped into some strange dream, the debilitating fears that gripped me yesterday somehow forgotten in a moment. Heat courses through me at a dangerous speed, my mind unable to grasp what my body clearly understands. There's so much I still need to say to her—so much I remember wanting to ask her. But when she steps out of her underwear and walks through the open bathroom door, into the shower, and then directly into my arms, I remember nothing.

My brain shuts down.

Her soft, naked body is pressed against every hard inch of mine, and suddenly I want nothing, nothing but this. The need is so great it actually feels like it might break me.

"Hey, handsome," she says, peering up at me. She runs her hands down my back, then lower. I can hear her smile. "You look too good in here to be all by yourself."

I can't speak.

She takes my hand, still smiling, and rests it against her breast before slowly guiding it down her body; she's showing me exactly what she wants from me. How she wants it.

But I already know.

I know where she wants my hands. I know where she wants my mouth. I know where she wants me most of all.

I take her into my arms, hitching her leg around my thigh before I kiss her, breaking her open. She's so soft, slick, and eager in my arms, kissing me back with an urgency that drives me wild. I tilt her head back as I break away, kissing her neck, then lower; slowly, carefully, replacing my hands with my mouth everywhere on her body. Her desperate, anguished sounds send shock waves of pleasure through me, setting me on fire. She reaches behind her, searching for purchase against the tile wall, her back arching with pleasure.

I love the way she loses herself with me, the way she lets go, trusting me completely with her needs, her pleasure. I never feel closer to her than when we're so entwined, when there's nothing but openness and love between us.

She touches me then, gently wraps her hand around me, and I squeeze my eyes shut, hardly able to contain the sound I make, low in my throat. All I can think in this moment is that I don't want this to be over; I want to be trapped in here for hours, her slick body against mine, her voice in my ear begging me, as she is now, to make love to her.

"Please," she says, still touching me. "Aaron—"

I sink down, without warning, onto my knees. Ella steps

back, confused for all of a second before her eyes widen with understanding.

"Come here, love."

Ella is hesitant at first. I feel her sudden shyness, desire, and self-consciousness colliding, and I study her as she stands there, the sheen of her wet curves in this light, her long dark hair painted to her skin. Hot drops of water race down her breasts, skim her navel. She's dripping wet, so gorgeous I hardly know what to do with myself.

She makes her way over to me slowly, her cheeks pink with heat, her eyes dark with need. I intercept her once she's standing in front of me, planting my hands around her hips. I look up at her in time to see her blush, a moment of self-consciousness gone in seconds. She's soon gasping my name, her hands in my hair, at the back of my neck. She's already so wet, so ready for me; the sight of her—the taste of her—it's too much. I feel like I'm detaching from my mind as I watch her lose herself. I can feel her legs shaking as she cries out for more, for *me*, and when she comes she stifles her scream in my hair. I'm on my feet a moment later, capturing the last of her cries with my mouth, kissing her as she trembles in my arms, her harsh breaths slowing down. Ella reaches for me even then, touches me until I'm blind with pleasure. She pushes me, gently, up against the wall, kissing my throat, running her hands down my chest, my torso, and then she sinks to her knees in front of me, taking me into her mouth—

I make a tortured sound, grasping at the wall, hardly able

to breathe. The pleasure is white-hot; all-encompassing. I can't think around it. I can hardly see straight. And for a moment I think I've actually lost my mind, separated from my body.

"Ella," I gasp.

"I want you," she says, breaking away, her words hot against my skin. "Please—now—"

My heart still pounding in my chest, I step aside.

Turn off the shower.

Ella startles, surprised even as she gets to her feet. I step past her to grab a towel for each of us and she accepts hers with some confusion, refusing to dry herself off.

"But—"

I scoop her up without a word and she squeaks, half laughing as I carry her over to the single bed in our room. I lay her down carefully, and she looks up at me, eyes wide with wonder, her wet hair plastered to her skin, water dripping everywhere. I couldn't care less if we flooded this room.

I join her on the bed, carefully straddling her damp, gleaming body before leaning down to kiss her, this need so brutal it's almost indistinguishable from anguish. I touch her while I kiss her, stroking her slowly at first, then deeper, more urgent. She whimpers against my mouth, urging me closer, lifting her hips.

I move inside her with painstaking slowness, the pleasure so profound it seems to sever my connection to reality.

"God, you feel so good," I say, hardly recognizing the ragged sound of my own voice. "I can't believe you're mine."

She only moans my name in response, her arms wrapped tight around my neck as she pulls me closer.

I can feel her growing torment, her need for release as great as my own. We find a rhythm as we move. Ella hooks her legs around my waist, and she doesn't stop kissing me; my mouth, my cheeks, my jaw—any part of me she can reach—her feverish touches interrupted only by desperate pleas begging me for more—faster, harder—

"I love you," she says desperately. "I love you so much—"

I let go when I feel her come apart, losing myself in the moment with a stifled cry, my body seizing as it succumbs to this, the most acute form of pleasure.

I bury my face in her chest, listening to the sound of her racing heart for only a moment before disengaging myself, for fear of crushing her. Somehow the two of us manage, just barely, to squeeze in together on the narrow bed.

Ella tucks herself into my side, pressing her face against my neck, and I reach for the insubstantial covers, drawing them up around us. She grazes my chest with the tips of her fingers, drawing patterns, and this single action ignites a low heat deep inside me.

I could do this all day.

I don't care what happened yesterday. I don't need an explanation. None of it seems to matter anymore, not when she's here with me. Not when her naked body is wrapped up in mine, not when she draws her hands along my skin, touching me with a tenderness that tells me everything I need to know.

All I want is this. Her.

Us.

I don't even realize I've fallen asleep until her voice startles me awake.

"Aaron," she whispers.

It takes me a moment to open my eyes, to find my voice. I turn toward her as if in a dream, pressing a soft kiss to her forehead. "Yes, love?"

"There's something I want to show you."

NINE

The morning is cool and serene, everything limned in golden light. Touches of dew dot leaves and grass, the sun still stretching itself into the sky. The air is fresh with scents I cannot adequately describe; it's an amalgam of early morning fragrances, the familiar smell of the world shuddering awake. That I notice these things at all is unusual; it is clear, even to me, that my mood is greatly improved.

Ella is holding my hand.

She's been buoyant this morning. She got dressed even more quickly than I did, tugging me out the door with an enthusiasm that almost made me laugh.

Winston, who we discover waiting for us just outside the medical tent, possesses a range of emotions diametrically opposed. He says nothing when Ella and I approach, first taking in the two of us, then glancing at his watch.

"Hey, Winston," Ella says, still beaming. "What are you doing here?"

"Who, me?" He points at himself, feigning shock. "Oh, nothing. Just waiting out here for this jackass"—he shoots me a dark look—"for over an hour."

"What? Why?" Ella frowns. "And don't call him a jackass."

I process this exchange with some confusion. I'd not

realized until just that moment how much I'd been hoping Winston's appearance at my door had something to do with Ella.

I see now that it does not.

"Winston came to our room this morning," I explain to her. "He told me he had . . . a surprise for me."

Ella's frown deepens. "A surprise?"

"*An hour ago*," Winston adds angrily.

"Yes," I say, meeting his eyes. "An hour ago."

He visibly clenches his jaw. "You really are the worst, you know that? I mean, everyone is always telling me that you're the worst—not that I've ever doubted it—but wow, this morning has just proven to me how completely self-absorbed you are. I can't believe I even offered to come get—"

"Winston." Ella's voice is quiet, carefully controlled, but her anger is loud. I turn to look at her, not surprised, exactly, but—

Yes, surprised.

I'm still unfamiliar with this dynamic. I'm still not used to someone taking my side.

"Look," she says. "Warner might be too nice to say anything when you talk to him like that—"

Winston sounds for a moment like he's choking.

"—but I'm not. So don't. Not only because it's awful, but because you're wrong."

Winston is still staring at Ella, dumbfounded. "I'm sorry— You think he's *too nice* to say anything? You think the reason Warner gets all quiet and gives people death stares is because he's *too nice*? To say anything?" Winston glances at me. *"Him?"*

I am smiling.

Ella is indignant, Winston is furious, and I am smiling. Very nearly laughing.

"Yes," Ella says, refusing to back down. "You guys are too comfortable bullying him."

Winston looks around himself a moment, for all the world as if he's entered some alternate universe. He opens his mouth to say something, looks at me, looks away, and then crosses his arms.

"You heard what he was like, right?" he finally says to Ella. "When you were gone? You heard all the stories about how h—"

"Yes," she says, her voice darker now. "I heard exactly what happened."

"And? So you know about all the people he murdered and how horrible he was to everyone and how he made a ton of people here cry and how Nouria nearly shot him for it—and you think *we* are the ones bullying *him*? That's what you think is happening here?"

"Clearly."

"And you," Winston says, turning to face me, his eyes narrowing with barely suppressed anger. "You agree with this assessment of your character?"

I smile wider. "Yes."

"Wow, you really are an asshole."

"Winston—"

"He made me wait out here for an *hour*! And this was after I told him I had a surprise for him, and after he slammed the door in my face—multiple times." Winston shakes his head. "You should've heard him. He's so scathing—so rude—"

"Hey, what the hell is going on over here?" Kenji is stalking toward us. "And where have *you* been?" he says to Ella. "We're all waiting for you guys!"

"Waiting for us?" I ask. "For what?"

Kenji throws up his arms in frustration. "Oh my God. You haven't told him yet?" he says to Ella. "What are you waiting for? Listen, I thought this idea was dumb to begin with, but now it's just getting ridiculous—"

"I was going to tell him this morning," she says, tensing. "I just haven't had a chance yet. We've been busy—"

"I bet you were, princess," Kenji says, a muscle ticking in his jaw. "Why is your hair wet?"

"I took a shower."

"You took a shower," he says, eyes narrowing. "Really."

"Okay— What is going on?" I ask, glancing between Ella and the others as a familiar dread moves up my spine. "Is this about the surprise?"

"The surprise?" Kenji is confused only a moment before understanding alights in his eyes. He looks at Winston. "Wait—I thought we sent you to go get him an *hour* ago?"

Winston explodes. *"This is exactly what I've been trying to say—* This son of a bitch made me wait outside the MT for an hour, even though I was perfectly nice to him, despite my better judgment—"

"Fucking hell," Kenji mutters angrily, pushing his hands through his hair. "As if we didn't have enough going on today." He turns to me. "You made Winston wait an entire hour just to give you the damn dog?"

"The dog?" I frown. "*The dog* is the surprise? How is it a surprise if I already know it exists?"

"Wait, what dog?" Ella looks at me, then at the others. "You mean the dog from yesterday?"

"Yeah." Kenji sighs. "Yara took the dog last night. She gave him a bath, scrubbed him up. She got him a collar and everything. She really wanted it to be a surprise for Warner and made us promise not to say anything about it. The dog is wearing a stupid bow on his head right now."

Ella has stiffened beside me. "Who's Yara?"

Her faint, almost undetectable note of jealousy—*possessiveness*—only cements my smile in place.

"You know Yara," Kenji says to Ella. "Redhead? Tall? Runs the school group? You've talked to her—"

Kenji catches sight of my face and cuts himself off.

"And what the hell are you smiling about? You've messed up our entire schedule, dickhead. We're an hour behind on everything now, all becau—"

"*Stop*," Ella says angrily. "Stop calling him names. He's not a dickhead. He's not a jackass. He's not self-absorbed. I don't know why you guys think it's okay to just say whatever terrible things you want about him—to his face—as if he's made of stone. You all do it. You all insult him over and over again and he just takes it—he doesn't even say anything—and somehow you've convinced yourselves it's okay. Why? He's a real, flesh-and-blood person. Why don't you care? Why don't you think he has feelings? What the hell is wrong with you?"

My smile is gone in an instant.

I experience a strange pain then, a sensation not unlike dissolving slowly from the inside. This feeling sharpens to a point, piercing me.

I turn to look at Ella.

She seems to sense the change in me; for a moment, they all do.

I feel a vague mortification at that, at the realization that I've somehow exposed myself. The proceeding silence is brief but torturous, and when Ella wraps her arms around my waist, hugging me close even in the midst of all this, I hear Winston clear his throat.

Tentatively, I lift a hand to her head, drawing it slowly down her hair. I worry, sometimes, that my love for her will expand beyond the limitations of my body, that it will one day kill me with its heft.

Kenji averts his eyes.

He is subdued when he says, "Yeah. Um, anyway, last I checked, the dog was in the dining tent, eating breakfast with everyone."

Another awkward beat, and Winston sighs. "Should I go get Yara? Do we even have time?"

"I don't think so," Kenji says. "I think we should tell her to keep the dog until after."

"After what?" I ask, trying to read the maelstrom of emotions around me and failing. "What's going on?"

Kenji blows out a breath. He looks exhausted. "J, you have to tell him."

She pulls away from me, panicked in an instant. "But I had a plan—I was going to take him there first—"

"We don't have time for this, princess. You waited too long, and now it's officially a problem. Tell him what's happening."

"Right now? While you're standing here?"

"Yes."

"No way." She shakes her head. "You have to at least give us some privacy."

"Absolutely not." Kenji crosses his arms. "I've given you tons of privacy, and you've proven you can't be trusted. If I leave you two alone together you'll either end up in bed or accomplish nothing, neither of which are conducive to our goals."

"Was that really necessary?" I say, irritated. "Did you really feel the need to comment on our private life?"

"When it costs us an hour of our lives, *yes*," Winston says, moving, in an act of solidarity, to stand next to Kenji. He even crosses his arms against his chest, matching Kenji's stance.

"Go ahead." He nods at Ella. "Tell him."

Ella looks nervous.

Winston and Kenji are an irritated, impatient audience; they stare us down, unrelenting, and I don't even know whether to be angry about it—because the truth is, I want to know what's going on, too. I want Ella to tell me what's happening.

I look from her to them, my heart pounding in my chest. I have no idea what she's about to say. No idea whether this revelation will be good or bad—though her nerves seem to indicate something is wrong. I brace myself as I watch her take a deep breath.

"Okay," she says, exhaling. "Okay." Another quick breath and she remembers to look at me, this time pasting an anxious smile on her face. "So—I didn't want to tell you like this, but I'd been thinking for a little while about how to do this in the best possible way, because I wanted everything to be *right*, you know? Right for both of us—and also, I didn't want it be anticlimactic. I didn't want this big thing to happen and then it was just, like, we go back to the status quo—I wanted it to feel special—like something was going to change—and I'm sorry I didn't tell you sooner, it was supposed to be a surprise, but it just wasn't ready in time, and if I'd told you about it, it wouldn't have been a surprise anymore, and Kenji kept insisting that I tell you anyway but I just—I'm sorry about yesterday, by the way, and I'm sorry about Nouria—I've been planning this whole thing with her since I woke up, practically, but she wasn't supposed to say anything to you, and she *knows* she wasn't supposed to say anything to you, because she and I had an agreement that I was supposed to tell you what was going on but yesterday I didn't know exactly what was going to happen and I was waiting for more information because we were still trying really hard to make everything work in time but I know how important it is to you t—"

"Jesus fucking Christ," Winston mutters.

Kenji shouts: *"You two are getting married today."*

I turn sharply, stunned, to look at them.

"Kenji, what the hell—"

"You were taking too long—"

"We're getting married today?" I turn back to meet Ella's eyes, my heart pounding now for an entirely new reason. A better reason. *"We're getting married today?"*

"Yes," she says, blushing fiercely. "I mean—only if you want to."

I smile at her then, smile so wide I start laughing, disbelief rendering me foreign even to myself.

I hardly recognize this sound.

The sensations moving through my body right now—it's hard to explain. The relief flooding my veins is intoxicating; I feel as if someone punched a hole through my chest in the best possible way. This is some kind of madness.

I'm trying, but I can't stop laughing.

"Huh," says Winston quietly. "I didn't even know his face could do that."

"Yeah," Kenji says. "It's super weird the first time you see it."

"I can't look away. I'm trying to look away and I can't. It's like if a baby was born with a full set of teeth."

"Yes! *Exactly*. It's exactly like that!"

"But nice, too."

"Yeah." Kenji sighs. "Nice, too."

"Hey, did you know he had dimples? I didn't know he had dimples."

"C'mon, man, that's old news—"

"Could you two just—please—*be quiet* for a second?" Ella says, squeezing her eyes shut. "Just for one second?"

Kenji and Winston mime zipping their mouths shut before taking a step back, holding their hands up in surrender.

Ella bites her lip before meeting my eyes.

"So," she says. "What do you think?" She clasps, unclasps her hands. "Are you busy this morning? There's still something I want to show you—something I've been working on for the last few—"

I take her in my arms and she laughs, breathlessly, just until she meets my eyes. Her smile is soon replaced by a look—a softness in her expression that likely mirrors my own. I can still feel the outline of that little velvet box against my leg; I've been carrying it with me everywhere, too afraid to leave it behind, too afraid to lose hope.

"I love you," I whisper.

When I kiss her I breathe her in, inhaling the scent of her skin as I draw my hands down her back, pulling her tighter. Her response is immediate; her small hands move up my chest to claim my face, holding me close as she deepens the kiss, standing on tiptoe as she slowly twines her arms around my neck.

The pilot light in my body catches fire.

I break away reluctantly, and only because I remember we have an audience. Still, I press my forehead to hers, keeping her close.

I'm smiling again. Like a common idiot.

"Okay, well, that took a gross turn."

"Is it over yet?" Kenji asks. "I had to close my eyes."

"I don't know. I think it might be over, but if I were you I'd keep my eyes shut for another minute just in case—"

"Can you two keep your commentary to yourselves?" I say, pivoting to face them. "Is it so impossible for you to just be happy for—"

The words die in my throat.

Winston and Kenji are both bright-eyed and beaming, the two of them failing to fight back enormous smiles.

"Congratulations, man," Kenji says softly.

His sincerity is so unexpected it strikes me before I've had a chance to armor myself, and the consequences leave me reeling.

An unfamiliar, overwhelming heat erupts in my head, in my chest, pricking the whites of my eyes.

Ella takes my hand.

I can't help but study Kenji's face; I'm astonished by the kindness there, the happiness he does nothing to hide. It becomes more obvious by the moment that he's played a larger role in executing Ella's plans than I might've suspected, and I experience the truth then—feel it clearly, for the first time—the realization like a physical jolt.

Kenji genuinely wants me to be happy.

"Thank you," I say to him.

He smiles, but it's only a flicker of movement. Everything else is in his expression, in the tight nod he gives me by way of response.

"Anytime," he says quietly.

There's a beat of silence, broken only by the sound of Winston sniffing.

"All right, okay, that was a really beautiful moment, but you guys need to knock it off before I start crying," he says, laughing even as he tugs off his glasses to rub at his eyes. "Besides, we still have a shit ton of work to do."

"Work," I say, searching the sky for the sun. "Of course." It can't be much later than eight in the morning, but I'm usually at my desk much earlier. "I'll need to make a quick stop at the command center. How long do you think we'll be gone today? I have to reschedule some calls. There are time-sensitive materials I'm supposed to deliver today, and if I—"

"Not that kind of work," Kenji says, a strange smile on his face. "You don't need to worry about that today. It's all been taken care of."

"Taken care of?" I frown. "How?"

"Juliette already notified everyone last night. Obviously we can't check out of work completely, but we've divvied up today's responsibilities. We're all going to take shifts." He hesitates. "Not you, two, obviously. Both your schedules have been cleared for the day."

Somehow, this is a greater surprise than everything else. If our schedules have been cleared, that means today wasn't some spur-of-the-moment decision. It means things didn't just serendipitously align in time to make it happen.

This was orchestrated. Premeditated.

"I don't think I understand," I say slowly. "As much as I appreciate the time off, this shouldn't take much more than an hour. We only need an officiant and a couple of witnesses. Ella doesn't even have a dress. Nouria said there was no time to make food, or a cake, or even to spare people to help set up, so it won't—"

Ella squeezes my hand, and I meet her eyes.

"I know we'd agreed to do something really small," she says softly. "I know you weren't expecting much. But I thought you might like this better."

I stare at her, dumbfounded. "Like *what* better?"

As if on cue, Brendan pops his white-blond head around a corner. "Morning, everyone! All right to bring everyone through? Or do you lot need another minute?"

Winston lights up at the sight of him, assuring Brendan that we need just a few more minutes.

Brendan says, "Roger that," and promptly disappears.

I turn to Ella, my mind whirring.

Save the birthday cake she surprised me with last month, I have very little in my life to offer me a frame of reference for this experience. My brain is at war with itself, understanding—while incapable of understanding—what now seems obvious. Ella has organized something elaborate.

In secret.

All of her earlier evasiveness, her half-truths and missing explanations—my fear that she'd been hiding something from me—

Suddenly everything makes sense.

"How long have you been planning this?" I ask, and Ella visibly tenses with excitement, emanating the kind of joy I've only ever felt in the presence of small children.

It nearly takes my breath away.

She wraps her arms around my waist, peering up at me. "Do you remember when we were on the plane ride home," she says, "and the adrenaline wore off, and I started kind of losing my mind? And I kept looking at the bone sticking out my leg and screaming?"

Of all things, this was not what I was expecting her to say.

"Yes," I say carefully. I have no interest in recalling the events of that plane ride. Or discussing them. "I remember."

"And do you remember what I said to you?"

I look away, sighing as I stare at a point in the distance. "You said you couldn't wear a wedding dress with part of your bone sticking out."

"Yeah," she says, and laughs. "Wow. I was pretty out of it."

"It's not funny," I whisper.

"No," she says, drawing her hands up my back. "No, it's not funny. But it was strange, how nothing was really making sense in my head. We'd just been through hell, but all I could think as I stared at myself was how impractical it was to be bleeding so much. I told you I couldn't marry you if the bleeding didn't stop, because then I'd get blood all over my dress, and your suit, and then we'd both just be covered in blood, and everything we touched would get bloody. And you"—she takes a deep breath—"you said you'd marry me right then. You said you'd marry me with my bleeding teeth, with a visibly broken leg, with dried blood on my face, with blood dripping from my ears."

I flinch at that, at the memory of what my father put her through. What her own parents did to her. Ella suffered and sacrificed so much for this world—all to bring The Reestablishment to its knees. All because she cared so much about this planet, and the people in it.

I feel suddenly ill.

What I hate, perhaps more than anything else, is that it doesn't stop. The demands on her body never stop. It doesn't seem to matter what side of history we're on; good or evil, everyone asks for more of her. Even now, after the fall of The Reestablishment, the people and their leaders *still* want more from her. They don't seem to care that she's only one person, or that she's already given so much. The more she gives, the more they require, and the quicker their gratitude shrivels up, the desiccated remains of which become something else altogether: expectation. If it were up to them, they'd keep taking from her until they've bled her dry—and I will never allow that to happen.

"Aaron."

Finally, I meet her eyes. "I meant what I said, love."

"I was hideous."

"You have never been hideous."

"I was a monster." She smiles as she says this. "I had that huge gash in my arm, the skin on my hands had split open, my nose wouldn't stop bleeding, my eyes wouldn't stop bleeding. I even had a freshly sutured finger. I was Frankenstein's monster. You remember? From that book—"

"Ella—please— We don't have to talk about this—"

"And I couldn't stop screaming," she says. "I was in so much pain, and I was so upset that I wouldn't stop bleeding, and I kept saying the craziest things, and you just sat next to me and listened. You answered every ridiculous question I asked like I wasn't completely out of my mind. *For hours.* I still remember, Aaron. I remember everything you said to me. Even after I passed out I heard you, on a loop, in my dreams. It was like your voice got caught in my head." She pauses. "I can only imagine what that experience must've been like for you."

I shake my head. "It wasn't about me. My experience doesn't matter—"

"Of course it does. It matters to *me*. You don't get to be the only one who worries about the person you love. I get to do that, too," she says, breaking away to better look me in the eye. "You spend so much time thinking about what's best for me. You're always worried about my safety and my happiness and the things I might need. Why don't I get to do that for you? Why don't I get to think about your happiness?"

"I am happy, love," I say quietly. "You make me happy."

She looks away at that, but when she meets my eyes again, she's fighting tears. "But if you could marry me however you wanted, you'd choose to do it differently, wouldn't you?"

"Ella," I whisper, tugging her back into my arms. "Sweetheart, why are you crying? I don't care about having a wedding. It doesn't matter to me. I'll marry you as you are right now, in the clothes we're wearing, right where we're standing."

"But if you *could* do it however you wanted, you'd do it differently," she says, looking up at me. "You'd do it better than that, wouldn't you?"

"Well— Yes—" I falter. "I mean, if it were a different world, maybe. If things were different for us, if we had more time, or more resources. And maybe one day we'll have a chance to do it over again, but right now all I—"

"No." She shakes her head. "I don't want to do it over again. I don't want you to look back on our wedding day as a placeholder for something else, or for what might've been. I want us to do it right the first time. I want to walk down an aisle to reach you. I want you to see me in a pretty dress. I want someone to take our picture. I want you to have that. You deserve to have that."

"But—how—"

I look up, distracted by the sounds of movement, voices. A crowd of people is swarming, moving toward us. Nazeera and Brendan lead the charge; Lily and Ian and Alia and Adam and James and Castle and Nouria and Sam and dozens of others—

They're all holding things: bouquets of flowers and covered trays of food and colorful boxes and folded linens and—

My blood pressure seems to plummet at the sight, leaving me dangerously light-headed. I take a sharp breath, try to clear my head. When I speak, I hardly recognize my voice.

"Ella, what did you do?"

She only smiles at me, eyes shining with feeling.

"How did you find so many flowers? Where—"

"All right," Winston says, holding up his hands. He sniffs, twice, and I see then that his eyes are red. "No more divulging secrets. We're done here."

Kenji, I notice, is looking determinedly away from all of us.

He clears his throat then, still staring at the sky when he says, "For what it's worth, bro, I tried to get her to tell you. I don't approve of this whole surprise-wedding nonsense. I told her—I said, if it were me, I'd want to know." Finally, Kenji meets my eyes. "But she wouldn't listen. She said it had to be a surprise. I said, *You're going to go back to your room tonight smelling like paint, and he's going to know! The man is not an idiot!* And she was like blah blah blah he's not going to know, blah blah blah, I'm the queen of the world, blah blah—"

"KENJI."

"What?"

Ella's fists are clenched. She looks like she might punch him in the face. "Please. Stop speaking."

"Why?" Kenji looks around. "What'd I say?"

"Paint," I say, frowning as I remember. "Of course. I thought you smelled like something faintly chemical last night. I wasn't sure what it was, though."

"What?" Ella says, crestfallen. "How? I thought you were asleep."

I shake my head, smiling now, though mostly for her benefit. Ella's guilt is palpable, and multiplying quickly.

"What was the paint for?" I ask.

"Nope!" Winston claps his hands together. "We're not doing that right now! You guys ready to get started? Good. Kenji and I will lead the way."

TEN

Ella is holding my hand like a lifeline, grinning as we forge an unfamiliar path through the Sanctuary. Her happiness is so electric it's contagious. I feel heavy with it, overwhelmed by it. I don't even think my body knows what to do with this much of it.

But seeing her like this—

It's impossible to describe what it does to me to see her so happy, smiling so wide she can hardly speak. I only know that I never want to do anything to make it stop.

We're following Kenji and Winston, both of whom were quickly joined by their counterparts, Nazeera and Brendan, while the rest of the crowd follows close behind. I seem to be the only one of us who doesn't know where we're going, and Ella still refuses to tell me anything more about our destination.

"Will you at least tell me whether we're leaving the Sanctuary?" I ask.

She smiles up at me. "Yes and no."

I frown. "Are we going somewhere to see the thing you wanted to show me? Or is this something else?"

Her smile grows bigger. "Yes and no."

"I see," I say, squinting into the distance. "So you're torturing me on purpose."

"Yes," she says, poking me in the stomach. "And no."

I shake my head, laughing a little, and she pokes me in the stomach again.

"Ow," I say quietly.

Ella beams before wrapping her arms around my waist, hugging me as we walk, not seeming to care at all that she stumbles every few steps. I'm so incomprehensibly happy I seem to have misplaced most of my brain cells. I can hardly gather my thoughts.

After a moment, Ella says, "You know, it's not much fun to poke you in the stomach. It's not even possible, really, to poke hard muscle." She slides her hand up under my shirt, then slowly down my torso. "This whole thing would work much better if you had some body fat."

I take a steadying breath. "I'm sorry to disappoint you."

"I never said I was disappointed," she says, still smiling. "I love your body."

Her words conjure a simmering heat somewhere deep inside me. I tense as she draws patterns along my skin, her fingers grazing my navel before moving slowly up again, tracing lines with excruciating care.

I finally cover her hand with my own.

"That," I say, "is very distracting."

"What is?" She's not even looking at the path ahead anymore. One of her arms is wrapped around my waist, and the

111

other is tucked unabashedly under my shirt. "This?" She drags her hand across my abs, moving steadily downward. "Is this distracting?"

I inhale. "Yes."

"What about this?" she says, staring up at me, the picture of innocence as her free hand travels lower, then slips just underneath my waistband. "Is this distracting?"

"Ella."

"Yes?"

I laugh, but the sound is breathless. Nervous. It's a struggle to maintain the control necessary to keep my body from announcing to everyone exactly what I would rather be doing right now.

"Do you want me to stop?" she asks.

"No."

She smiles wider. "Good, because—"

"If you two are going to be disgusting on your wedding day," Kenji says over his shoulder, "could you at least *whisper*? It's close quarters in this crowd, okay? No one wants to hear your filthy conversations."

"Yeah," Nazeera says, turning to look at us. "No cute talk, either. Cute talk is highly discouraged on any day, but especially on your wedding day."

Ella's hand is gone from my body in an instant.

She turns to face them, the moment all but forgotten; I, on the other hand, need a minute. The effect she has on my nerves takes longer to dissipate.

I exhale slowly.

"I'm starting to think you two might be turning into the same person," Ella says. "And I'm not sure I mean that as a compliment."

Kenji and Nazeera laugh at that, Kenji drawing an arm around Nazeera's waist as they walk, pulling her closer. She leans into him, planting a brief kiss at the base of his jaw.

Kenji's provocations have grown innocuous in recent weeks. His bite is more habit than harmful, as he's in no position to criticize. He and Nazeera are as inseparable as is possible these days, the two of them ensconced in darkened corners at every available opportunity. To be fair, we're all lacking in privacy right now; very few people have their own rooms at the moment, which means we're not the only ones engaging in public displays of affection.

Kenji and Nazeera seem truly happy, though.

I've not known Kenji a particularly long time, but Nazeera—I never thought I'd see her like this.

I suppose she might say the same about me.

"You know, technically, you two shouldn't even be together right now," Winston says, swiveling to face us. He walks backward as he says, "The bride and groom can't just hang out together on their wedding day. Tradition frowns upon it."

"Excellent point," Brendan adds. "And as they're both such pure, innocent souls, we wouldn't want them to risk accidental, indecent skin-to-skin contact."

"Yeah, I think it might be too late for that," Kenji says.

"Seriously?" Brendan and Nazeera say at the same time.

Brendan laughs, but Nazeera turns sharply around to look at Ella, whose responding blush all but confirms their suspicions.

"Wow," Nazeera says after a moment, nodding. "Nice. You have interesting priorities."

"*Oh my God*," Ella says, covering her face with her hand. "Sometimes I really hate you guys."

I decide to change the subject.

"Will we be arriving at this mysterious destination soon?" I ask. "We've been walking for so long I'm beginning to wonder whether I'll need international clearance."

"Is this guy serious?" Winston calls back, exasperated. "It's been *maybe* five minutes."

"Sprinting two miles—uphill, in the heat, in a suit—and he doesn't break a sweat," Kenji says. "Wouldn't even let me rest for thirty-seconds. But *this*—yeah, this is too much for him. Makes sense."

"Okay, you can ignore them," Ella says, taking my hand again. "We're pretty close now." I feel her enthusiasm building anew, her eyes brightening as she peers ahead.

"So—what changed yesterday?" I ask her. "To make all this happen?"

Ella looks up. "What do you mean?"

"Yesterday Nouria told me that, for a number of different reasons, it was basically out of the question for us to have a wedding. But today"—I glance around us, at the mass of people sacrificing hours of their work and life to help organize this event—"those issues no longer seem to be relevant."

"Oh," Ella says, and sighs. "Yeah. Yesterday was a mess. I really didn't want to postpone things, but there were just so many different disasters to deal with. Losing our clothes was one obstacle, but trying to host the wedding at night was proving a logistical nightmare. I realized we could either get married last night and have to compromise on almost everything, or push it by a day, and *maybe*, just maybe, be able to do it right—"

"A day?" I frown. "Nouria made it seem like it might be months before we could reschedule. She made it sound functionally impossible."

"*Months?*" Ella stiffens. "Why would she say that?"

"You must've really pissed her off," Kenji says, his laughter echoing. "Nouria knew Juliette wouldn't have postponed the wedding that long. She was probably just torturing you."

"*Really.*" The revelation makes me scowl. Between her and Sam, I seem to have made two very powerful enemies.

"Hey—I'm sorry she said that to you," Ella says softly, hugging me from the side as we walk. I wrap my arm around her shoulders, holding her tight against me.

"I think Nouria leaned a little too hard into the cover story," she says. "I had no idea you thought we might be postponing the wedding that far into the future. I'm only now realizing that yesterday must've been pretty rough for you."

"It wasn't," I lie, gently cupping the back of her head,

my fingers threading through the silk of her hair. I study her face as she stares up at me, noticing then how the sun changes her eyes; her irises look more green in the light. Blue in the dark. "It was fine."

Ella doesn't buy this.

Her hands graze my hips as she draws away, lingering before she lets go. "I was so busy trying to make everything work that I didn't even—"

She cuts herself off, her emotions changing without warning.

"Hey," she says. "What's this?"

"What's what?"

"This," she says, gently prodding my pant leg in a manner that would disturb Kenji for weeks. "This box."

"*Oh.*"

I come to a sudden and complete stop, heart pounding as the crowd surges around us, several of them calling out congratulations as they pass. Someone sticks a homemade tiara on Ella's head at one point, which she accepts with a gracious nod before discreetly tugging it out of her hair.

They seem to know better than to touch me.

In the distance, I hear Winston clap his hands. "All right, everyone, we're basically here. Juliette, will you and Warner pl— Wait, where's Juliette?"

"I'm back here!"

"Why the hell are you back there?" Kenji cries.

I hear faint grumbling from Winston, more exasperated words from Kenji; all this is followed by soothing sounds made by their partners. The sequence would be comical if I were in any mood to laugh.

Instead, I have turned to stone.

"We'll be right there!" Ella reassures them. "You can start setting up without us!"

"Set up without you? If I find out this was your plan all along, princess, Nazeera is going to kick your ass."

"I absolutely won't," she calls out cheerfully. "In fact, I fully support the two of you tearing off each other's clothes, if that's what you've got planned!"

"Oh my God, Nazeera—"

"What?"

"Don't encourage them," Kenji and Winston shout at the same time.

"Why not?" Brendan says. "I think it's romantic."

They bicker a bit more while my mind spins. I feel the outline of the box against my leg more acutely than ever, a square spot of heat against my skin.

This is happening out of order.

I manage to comfort myself with the reminder that everything about us has unfolded in an unconventional way; I shouldn't be too surprised to discover that, here, too, things are not going to plan.

Then again, I didn't really have a plan.

In an ideal scenario, I would've proposed to her with the ring; she should've already had it on her finger. Instead, we are now fast approaching our actual wedding and I've yet to give it to her. And while it occurs to me that I could find a way to evade her curiosity right now, I'm not sure there's any point in prolonging it. I have no idea where we're going. I don't know what's going to happen next.

I might not even have time later to do this properly.

I swallow, hard, trying to force back my apprehension. I don't know why I'm so nervous.

That's not true.

I know why I'm nervous. I'm worried she's going to hate it, and I don't know what I'll do if she hates it. I suppose I'll have to return it. I'll have to marry her without a ring, acknowledging all the while that I am an idiot of astronomical proportions, one who couldn't even manage to pick out a decent ring for his fiancée.

This imagining inspires in me a wave of dread so severe I close my eyes against the force of it.

"Aaron," Ella says, and my eyes fly open, bringing me back to the present.

She is smiling at me.

Ella, I realize, already knows what's in the box.

Somehow, this makes me more nervous. I look around myself, searching for calm, and register a beat too late that we're all alone. The crowd has dispersed into the distance beyond us, and as I watch them disappear—their bodies growing smaller by the second—I recognize only then that I have no idea where we are.

I take stock of our surroundings: there are paved roads and sidewalks not far away, wilting trees planted at regular intervals. The air smells different—sharper—and the sun seems brighter, unencumbered by dense woods. I hear that familiar trill of birdsong and search the sky again, trying to orient myself. My mind searches itself for maps, blueprints, old information. This area looks less wild than the Sanctuary, stripped back. I feel quite certain we must be encroaching upon old, unregulated territory, but as we still appear to be within the boundary of Nouria's protections, that can't be possible. The lights that delineate our space from the outside world are clearly visible.

"Where are we?" I ask. For a moment, my nerves are forgotten. "This isn't—"

"We can get to that in just a second," Ella says, still smiling. She drops the homemade tiara to the ground and steps forward, drawing her hand slowly up my thigh, tracing a faint circle around the impression of the box. "But first, I feel like I have no choice but to make a terrible joke about finding something hard in your pants."

I drag a hand down my face, vaguely mortified. "Please don't."

Ella fights to be serious, biting her lip to keep from smiling. She mimes locking her mouth, tossing the key.

I actually laugh then, after which I sigh, staring for a moment into the distance.

"So. What's in the box?" she asks, her joy so bright it's blinding. "Is it for me?"

"Yes."

When I make no move to procure the object, she frowns. "Can I . . . have it?"

With great reluctance, I tug free the little velvet box from my pocket, clenching it tight for so long she finally reaches for my hand. Gently, she wraps her small fingers around my fist.

"Aaron," she says. "What's wrong?"

"Nothing." I take a deep breath. "Nothing is wrong. I just—" I force myself to open my palm to her, heart still pounding. "I really hope you like it."

She smiles as she takes the box. "I'm sure I'm going to love it."

"It's okay if you don't. You don't have to love it. If you hate it I can always get you something else—"

"You know, I'm not used to seeing you nervous like this." She tilts her head at me. "It's kind of adorable."

"I feel like an idiot," I say, trying and failing to smile. "Though I'm glad you find it entertaining."

She opens the box as I say this, giving me no time to brace myself before she gasps, her eyes widening in astonishment. She covers her mouth with one hand, her emotions so unrestrained I can hardly read them. There's too much all at once: shock, happiness, confusion—

The effort to say nothing nearly costs me my sanity.

"Where did you get this?" she says, finally dropping her hand away from her face. Carefully, she tugs the engagement ring free from its setting, examining it closely before staring up at me. "I've never seen anything like this."

"I had it made," I manage to say, my body still so tense

it's difficult to speak. She hasn't said whether she likes it, which means the vise around my chest refuses to disengage.

Still, I force myself to retrieve the glittering piece from her, taking her left hand in mine with great care. My own hands are miraculously steady as I slide the ring into place on her fourth finger.

The fit, as I knew it would be, is perfect.

I took the necessary measurements while she was heavily asleep, still recovering in the medical tent.

"You had it *made*?" Ella is staring at her hand, the ring refracting the light, shattering color everywhere. The center stone is large, but not garishly so, and suits her beautifully.

I think so, anyway.

I watch her as she studies the ring, turning her hand left and right. "How did you get it made?" she asks. "*When?* I thought there'd be a simple wedding band inside, I didn't think—"

"There is a wedding band inside. There are two rings."

She looks up at me then, and I see, for the first time, that her eyes are bright with tears. The sight cuts me straight through the heart but brings with it the hope of relief. It might be the only time in my life I've ever been happy to see her cry.

With great trepidation, Ella reopens the velvet box, slowly retrieving from its depths the wedding band.

She holds it up to the sky with a trembling hand, staring at its detail. The brushed gold band resembles a twig, so delicate it looks almost as if it were forged from thread. It glints in the sun, the two emerald leaves bright against the infinite branch.

She slips it onto her finger, gasping softly when it settles into place. It was designed to fit perfectly against the engagement ring.

"The leaves—are supposed to be—like us," I say, hearing how stupid it sounds when I say it out loud. How perfectly pedestrian.

I suddenly hate myself.

Still, Ella says nothing, and I can't hold the question in any longer. "Do you like it? If you don't like it I can always—"

She snaps the box shut and throws her arms around my neck, hugging me so tight I feel the damp press of her cheek against my jaw. She pulls back to pepper my face with kisses, half laughing as she does, swiping at her tears with shaking hands.

"How can you even ask me that?" she says. "I've never owned anything so beautiful in my whole life. I love these rings. I love them so much. And I know you probably didn't think about this when you had them made—because you wouldn't—but the emeralds remind me of your eyes. They're stunning."

I blink at that, surprised. "My eyes?"

"Yes," she says quietly, her expression softening. "And you're right. They *are* like us. We've been growing toward each other from the opposite sides of the same path since the beginning, haven't we?"

Relief hits me like an opiate.

I pull her into my arms, burying my face in her neck before I kiss her—softly at first—and our slow, searing touches quickly change into something else altogether. Ella is drawing her hand under my shirt again, my skin heating under her touch.

"I love you," she whispers, kissing my throat, my jaw, my chin, my lips. "And I never want to take these off." Her words are accompanied by a passion so profound I can hardly breathe around it. I close my eyes as the sensations build and spiral; the cold graze of her rings against my chest striking my skin like a match.

Desire soon shuts down my mind.

When we break apart I'm breathing hard, molten heat coursing through my veins. I'm imagining scenarios far too impractical to execute. Being with Ella this morning was like breaking a dam; I'd been so afraid to touch her while she was in recovery, and then terrified to overwhelm her in the days after. I'd wanted to make sure she was okay, that she took her time getting back to normal, at her own pace, without anyone crowding her personal space.

But now—

Now that she's ready—now that my body remembers this—it's suddenly impossible to get enough.

"I'm so glad you like the rings, love," I whisper against her mouth. "But I'm going to need to take back the band."

"What?" she says, pulling away. She stares at her hand, heartbroken in an instant. "Why?"

"Those are the rules." I'm still smiling when I touch her face, grazing her cheek with my knuckles. "I promise, after I give this ring to you today, I'll never ask for it back."

When still she makes no move, I reach, without looking, for the box clenched in her right fist.

She relinquishes the item with great reluctance, sighing as she steps back to slip the wedding band off her finger. I open the recovered box, presenting it to her, and after she settles the ring back into its nest I snap the lid shut, tucking the object safely back into my pocket.

My heart has grown ten sizes in the last several minutes.

"We should probably get going if you want to get this back," I say, touching her waist, then tugging her close. My lips are at her ear when I whisper: "I'm going to marry you today. And then I'm going to make love to you until you can't remember your name."

Ella makes a startled, breathless sound, her hands tightening in my shirt. She pulls me closer and kisses me, nipping my bottom lip before claiming my mouth, touching me now with a new desperation; a hunger still unmet. She presses her body against me, hard and soft soldered together, and I lose myself in it, in the intoxication of knowing just how much she wants this.

Me.

Her mouth is hot and sweet, her limbs heavy with pleasure. She drags her hand down the front of my pants and I make an anguished sound somewhere deep in my chest. I take her face in my hands as she touches me, kissing her deeper, harder, still unable to find relief. She seems to be torturing me on purpose—torturing both of us—knowing there's nothing we can do here, knowing there are people waiting for us—

"Ella," I gasp, the word practically a plea as I break away, trying and failing to cool my head, my thoughts. I can't walk back into a crowd right now, looking like this. I can't even think straight.

My thoughts are wild.

I want nothing more than to strip her bare. I want to fall to my knees and taste her, make her lose her mind with pleasure. I want her to beg before I make her come, right here, in the middle of nowhere.

"I really don't think you understand what you do to me, love," I say, trying to steady myself. "You have no idea how badly I want you. You have no idea what I want to do to you right now."

My words do not have the intended effect. Ella is not deterred.

Her desire seems to intensify, more in every second. That she could ever want me like this—that I could ever inspire in her the kind of need she inspires in me—

It still seems impossible.

And it's addicting.

"*You* have no idea," she says softly, "how you make me feel when you look at me like that."

I take a deep, unsteady breath when she touches me again, dragging my hands down her body before sliding a hand under her sweater, up the curve of her rib cage. She gasps as I skim the soft, heavy swell of her breasts, her body responding in an instant to my touch.

Her skin here, like everywhere, is like satin.

"God," I breathe. "I can never get enough of you."

Ella shakes her head even as she closes her eyes, surrendering to my hands. "Kenji was right," she says breathlessly. "We can't be left alone together."

I kiss her neck slowly, tasting her there until she moans, not enough to leave a mark. She reaches for me then, her own hands grasping for the button of my pants. In my delirium I let it happen, forgetting for a moment where we are or what we need to be doing until I feel her soft fingers wrap around me—a cool hand against my feverish skin—and my head nearly catches fire.

I'm moments away from losing my mind. I want to strip off her sweater. I want to unhook her bra. I want her to undress in front of me before I—

This is madness.

Common sense is returned to me only through a brutal, agonizing reclamation of self-control, just enough for me to place a hand over hers, forcing myself to breathe slowly.

"We can't do this here," I say, hating myself even as I say it. "Not here. Not now."

She looks around herself then as if emerging from a dream, the real world coming back into focus by degrees. I take advantage of her distraction to put myself to rights, stunned to realize I was only moments away from doing something reckless.

Ella's disappointment is palpable.

"I need to take you to bed, love," I say, my voice still rough with desire. "I need hours. Days. Alone with you."

She nods, her ring catching the light as she reaches for me, collapsing against my chest. "Yes. Please. I really hope you're not planning on falling asleep tonight."

I laugh at that, the sound still a bit shaky. "One day we'll have a proper bed," I say, kissing her forehead. "And then I doubt I will ever sleep again."

Ella jerks back suddenly.

Her eyes widen with something like comprehension, then delight. She nearly bounces up and down before taking my hand, and with only a sharp exclamation of excitement, she tugs me forward.

"Wait— Ella—"

"I still have something to show you!" she cries, and breaks off into a run.

I have no choice but to chase after her.

ELEVEN

At first, I hear only Ella's laughter, the effortless joy of a carefree moment. Her hair whips around her as she runs, streaming in the sun. I enjoy this sight more than I know how to explain; she runs through the several remaining feet of undeveloped land into the center of an abandoned street, all with the uninhibitedness of a child. I'm so entranced by this scene that it's a moment before I register the distant scream of an ungreased hinge: the repetition of steel abrading itself. My feet finally hit pavement as I follow her down the neglected road, the impact of my boots on the ground signifying the sudden change in place with hard, definitive thuds. The sun bears down on me as I run, surprising me with its severity, the light undiminished by cloud or tree cover. I slow down as the distant whine grows louder, and when the source of this keening finally comes into view, I skid to a sudden stop.

A playground.

Rusted and abandoned, a set of swings screeching as the wind pushes around their empty seats.

I've seen such things before; playgrounds were common in a time before The Reestablishment; I saw a great deal of them on my tours of old unregulated territory. They were built most often in areas where there existed large group-ings of homes. Neighborhoods.

Playgrounds were not known to be found at random near densely forested areas like the Sanctuary, nor were they built for no reason in the middle of nowhere.

Not for the first time, I'm desperate to understand where we are.

I wander closer to the rusting structure, surprised to feel a distinct lack of resistance when I step onto the haunted play area. The playground is built atop material that gives a bit when I walk; it seems to be made from something like rubber, surrounded otherwise by concrete pavers anchored by metal benches, paint peeling in sharp ribbons. There are long stretches of dirt beyond the borders, where no doubt grass and trees once thrived.

I frown.

This couldn't possibly be any part of the Sanctuary—and yet there's no question at all that we're still within Nouria's jurisdiction.

I look around then, searching for Ella.

I catch a glimpse of her before she disappears down yet another poorly paved road—the asphalt ancient and cracked—and silently berate myself for falling behind. I'm about to cross what appears to be the remains of an inter-section when suddenly she's back, her distant figure rushing into view before coming to a halt.

She noticed I was gone.

It's a small gesture—I realize this even as I react to

it—but it makes me smile nonetheless. I watch her as she spins around, searching the street for me, and I lift a hand to let her know where I am. When our eyes finally meet she jumps up and down, waving me forward.

"Hurry," she cries, cupping her mouth with her hands.

I clear the distance between us, analyzing my surroundings as I do. The old street signs have been vandalized so completely they're now rendered meaningless, but there remain a few traffic lights still hung at intervals. Relics of the old speaker system installed in the early days of The Reestablishment have survived as well, the ominous black boxes still affixed to lampposts.

People used to live here, then.

When I finally reach Ella, I take her hand, and she immediately tugs me forward, even as she's slightly out of breath. Running has always been harder for Ella than it is for me. Still, I resist her effort to drag me along.

"Love," I say. "Where are we?"

"I'm not going to tell you," she says, beaming. "Even though I have a feeling you've already figured it out."

"This is unregulated territory."

"Yes." She smiles brighter, then dims. "Well, sort of."

"But how—"

She shakes her head before attempting to pull me forward again, now with greater difficulty. "No explanations yet! Come on, we're almost there!"

Her energy is so effervescent it makes me laugh. I watch

her a moment as she struggles to move me, her effort not unlike that of a cartoon character. I imagine it must frustrate her not to be able to use her powers on me, but then I remind myself that Ella would never do something like that even if she could; she'd never overpower me just to get what she wanted. That's not who she is.

She is, and always has been, a better person than I will ever be.

I take her in then, her eyes glinting in the sun, the wind tousling her hair. She is a vision of loveliness, her cheeks flushed with feeling and exertion.

"Aaron," she says, pretending to be mad. I don't think it productive to tell her, but I find this adorable. When she finally lets go of my hand, she throws up her arms in defeat.

I'm smiling as I tuck a windblown hair behind her ear; her pretend anger dissipates quickly.

"You really don't want to tell me anything about where we're going?" I ask. "Not a single thing? I'm not allowed to ask even one clarifying question?"

She shakes her head.

"I see. And is there any particular reason why our destination is such a highly guarded secret?"

"That was a question!"

"Right." I frown, squinting into the distance. "Yes."

Ella puts her hands on her hips. "You're going to ask me another question, aren't you?"

"I just want to know how Nouria managed to draw

unregulated territory into her protection. I'd also like to know why no one told me she had plans to do such a thing. And why—"

"No, no, I can't answer those questions without spoiling the surprise." Ella blows out a breath, thinking. "What if I promise to explain everything when we get there?"

"How much longer until we get there?"

"Aaron."

"Okay," I say, fighting back a laugh. "Okay. No more questions."

"You swear?"

"I swear."

She makes an exclamation of delight before kissing me quickly on the cheek, and then takes my hand again. This time, I let her drag me forward, following her, without another word, onto an unmarked road.

The street curves as we go, unwilling even now to reveal our destination. We ignore the sidewalks, as cars aren't to be expected here, but it still feels strange to be walking down the center of a street, our feet following the faded yellow lines of another world, avoiding potholes as we go.

There are more trees here than I expected, more green leaves and patches of living grass than I thought we'd find. These are vestiges of another time, still managing to survive, somehow, despite everything. The limp greenery seems to multiply the farther we walk, the half-bare trees planted on either side of the pockmarked road clasping branches overhead to form an eerie tunnel around us. Sunlight shatters through the wooden webbing above, casting a kaleidoscope of light and shadow across our bodies.

I know we must be getting close to our destination when Ella's energy changes, her emotions a jumble of joy and nerves. It's not long before the dead road finally opens up onto an expansive view—and I come to a violent halt.

This is a residential street.

Just under a dozen houses, each several feet apart, separated by dead, square lawns. My heart pounds wildly in my chest, but this is nothing I haven't seen before. It's a vision of a bygone era; these homes, like so many others on unregulated turf, are in various states of decay, succumbing to time and weather and neglect. Roofs collapsing, walls boarded up, windows broken, front doors hanging from their hinges, all of them half-destroyed. It's like so many other neighborhoods around the continent, save one extraordinary difference.

In the center is a home.

Not a house—not a building—but a *home*, salvaged from the wreckage. It's been painted a simple, tasteful shade of white—not too white—its walls and roof repaired, the front door and shutters a pale sage green. The sight gives me déjà vu; I'm reminded at once of another house of a different vintage, in a different place. *Robin's-egg blue.*

The difference between them, however, is somehow palpable.

My parents' old house was little more than a graveyard, a museum of darkness. This house is bright with possibility, the windows big and brilliant, and beyond them: people. Familiar faces and bodies, crowding together in the front room. If I strain, I can hear their muted voices.

This must be some kind of dream.

The lawn is in desperate need of water, the single tree in the front yard withering slowly in the sun. There's a duo of rusty garbage bins visible in a side alley, where a surprise street cat languishes in a streak of sunlight. I can't recall the last time I saw a cat. I feel as if I've stepped into a time machine, into a vision of a future I was told I'd never have.

"Ella," I whisper. "What did you do?"

She squeezes my hand; I hear her laugh.

I turn slowly to face her, a wealth of feeling rising up inside me with a force so great it scares me.

"What is this?" I ask, hardly able to speak. "What am I looking at?"

Ella takes a deep breath, exhaling as she clasps her hands together. She's nervous, I realize.

This astonishes me.

"I had the idea a long time ago," she says, "but it wasn't workable back then. I always wanted us to be able to reclaim these old neighborhoods; it always seemed like such a waste to lose them altogether. We're still going to have to demolish most of them, because the majority are too far gone for repair, but that means we can redesign better, too—and it means we can tie it all into the new infrastructure package, creating jobs for people.

"I've been in talks with our newly contracted city planner,

by the way." She smiles tightly. "I never got to tell you about that yesterday. We're hoping to rebuild these areas in phases, prioritizing the transplantation of the disabled and the elderly and those with special needs. The Reestablishment did everything it could to throw anyone they deemed *unfit* into the asylums, which means none of the compounds they built made provisions for the old or infirm or all the orphans—which, I mean—of course, you already know all this." She looks sharply away at that, hugging herself tightly. When she looks up again I'm struck by the potency of her grief and gratitude.

"I really don't think I've said thank you enough for all that you've done," she says, her voice breaking as she speaks. "You have no idea how much it meant to me. Thank you. *So much.*"

She throws herself into my arms, and I hold her tight, still stunned into silence. I feel all her emotions at once, love and pain and fear, I realize, for the future. My heart is jackhammering in my chest.

Ella has always been deeply concerned with the well-being of the asylum inmates. After reclaiming Sector 45, she and I would talk late into the night about her dreams for change; she often said the first thing she'd do after the fall of The Reestablishment would be to find a way to reopen and staff the old hospitals—in anticipation of the immediate transfer of asylum residents.

While Ella was in recovery, I launched this initiative personally.

We've begun staffing the newly open hospitals not only with reclaimed doctors and nurses from the compounds but with supplies and soldiers from local sector headquarters all across the continent. The plan is to assess each asylum victim before deciding whether they need continued medical treatment and/or physical rehabilitation. Any healthy and able among them will be released back into the care of their living relatives, or else found safe accommodations.

Ella has thanked me for doing this a thousand times, and each time I've assured her that my efforts were nominal at best.

Still, she refuses to believe me.

"There's no one in the whole world like you," she says, and I can practically feel her heart beating between us. "I'm so grateful for you."

These words cause me an acute pain, a kind of pleasure that makes it hard to breathe. "I am nothing," I say to her. "If I manage to be anything, it is only because of you."

"Don't say that," she says, hugging me tighter. "Don't talk about yourself like that."

"It's true."

I never would've been able to get things done so quickly for her if Ella hadn't already won over the military contingent, a feat managed almost entirely through rumor and gossip regarding her treatment of the soldiers from my old sector.

During her brief tenure in 45, Ella gave soldiers leave to reunite with their families, allocated those with children

136

larger rations, and removed execution as a punishment for any infraction, minor or major. She regularly shrugs off these changes as if they were nothing. To her, they were casual declarations made over a meal, a young woman waving a fork around as she raged against the fundamental dignities denied our soldiers.

But these changes were radical.

Her effortless compassion toward even the lowest foot soldiers gained Ella loyalty across the continent. It took little work, in the end, to convince our North American infantry-men and -women to take orders from Juliette Ferrars; they moved quickly when I bade them to do so on her behalf.

Their superiors, however, have proven an altogether different struggle.

Even so, Ella doesn't see yet just how much power she wields, or how significantly her point of view changes the lives of so many. She refuses herself, as a result, any claim to credit; attributing her decisions to what she calls "a basic grasp of human decency." I tell her, over and over again, how rare it is to find any among us who've retained such decency. Even fewer remain who can look beyond their own struggles long enough to bear witness to the suffering of others; fewer still, who would do anything about it.

That Juliette Ferrars is incapable of seeing herself as an exception is part of what makes her extraordinary.

I take a deep, steadying breath as I hold her, still study-ing the house in the distance. I hear the muted sound of laughter, the bustle of movement. A door opens somewhere, then slams shut, unleashing sound and clamor, voices growing louder.

"Where do you want these chairs?" I hear someone shout, the proceeding answer too quiet to be intelligible.

Emotional tremors continue to wreck me.

They are setting up for our wedding, I realize.

In our house.

"No," Ella whispers against my chest. "It's not true. You deserve every good thing in the world, Aaron. I love you more every single day, and I didn't even think that was possible."

This declaration nearly kills me.

Ella pulls back to look me in the eye, now fighting tears, and I can hardly look at her for fear I might do the same.

"You never complain when I want to eat every meal with everyone. You never complain when we spend hours in the Q in the evening. You never complain about sleeping on the floor of our hospital room, which you've done every single night for the last fourteen nights. But I know you. I know it must be killing you." She takes a sharp breath, and suddenly she can't meet my eyes.

"You need quiet," she says. "You need space, and privacy. I want you to know that I know that—that I see you. I appreciate everything you do for me, and I see it, I see it every single time you sacrifice your comfort for mine. But I want to take care of you, too. I want to give you peace. I want to give you a home. With me."

There's a terrifying heat behind my eyes, a feeling I force

myself always to kill at all costs, and which today I am unable to defeat entirely. It's too much; I feel too full; I am too many things. I look away and take a sharp breath, but my exhalation is unsteady, my body unsteady, my heart wild.

Ella looks up, slowly at first, her expression softening at the sight of my face.

I wonder what she sees in me then. I wonder whether she's able to see right through me even now, and then I surprise myself for wondering. Ella is the only one who's ever bothered to wonder whether I'm more than I appear.

Still, I can only shake my head, not trusting myself to speak.

Ella experiences a sharp stab of fear in the intervening silence, and bites her lip before asking: "Was I wrong? Do you hate it?"

"Hate it?" I break away from her entirely at that, finding my voice only as a strange panic seizes me, making it hard for me to breathe. "Ella, I don't . . . I've done *nothing* to deserve you. The way you make me feel—the things you say to me— It's terrifying. I keep thinking the world will realize, any second now, how completely unworthy I am. I keep waiting for something horrible to happen, something to reset the scales and return me to hell, where I belong, and then all of this will just disappear. You'll just disappear. God, just thinking about it—"

Ella is shaking her head. "You and I— Aaron, people like us think good things will disappear because that's how it's always been. Good things have never lasted in our lives;

happiness has never lasted. And somehow we can only expect what we've experienced."

I'm sustaining full-blown anxiety now, my traitorous body shutting down, and Ella takes my hands, anchoring me.

I look into her eyes even as my heart races.

"But do you know what I've realized?" she says. "I've realized that we have the power to break these cycles. We can choose happiness for ourselves and for each other, and if we do it often enough, it'll become our new normal, displacing the past. Happiness will stop feeling strange if we see it every day."

"Ella—"

"I love you," she says. "I've always loved you. I'm not going anywhere."

I take her into my arms then, pulling her tightly against me, breathing in the familiar scent of her. When she's here, *right here*, it's so much easier to breathe. She's real when she's in my arms.

"I don't even know how to thank you for this," I whisper into her hair, closing my eyes against the heat in my head, in my chest. "You have no idea what it means to me, love. It's the greatest gift anyone has ever given me."

She laughs then, soft and gentle.

"Don't thank me yet," she says, peering up. "The house still needs a lot of work. The exterior is in pretty good shape now, but the inside is still kind of a disaster. We were only able to get one of the rooms ready in time, but it was—"

"*We?*" I lean back, frowning.

Ella laughs out loud at the look on my face. "Of course *we*," she says. "Did you think I did this all on my own? Everyone helped. They all gave up so much of their time to make this happen for you."

I shake my head. "If people helped, they did it for you," I point out. "Not me."

"They care about you, too, Aaron."

"That is a very generous lie," I say, smiling now.

"It's not a lie."

"It's possibly the biggest lie you've ever told."

"It's not! Even Ian helped. He taught me how to frame a wall—and he was so patient—and you know how he feels about me. Even Nouria helped. Well, especially Nouria. We couldn't have done any of this without Nouria."

I find this especially surprising, given her undisguised loathing of my existence. "She pulled this area into her protection? Just for me?"

Ella nods, then frowns. "Well. Yes. I mean, sort of. It's also part of a larger plan."

I smile wider at that. "Really," I say.

Nouria's involvement—and the involvement of the others—makes a great deal more sense if this project is in fact one small part of a broader initiative, though I keep this to myself. Ella seems incapable of believing how much everyone here hates me, and I don't relish disabusing her of this notion.

"We're going to build a campus for the Sanctuary," she explains, "and this is the first phase. We had scouts do a ton of site visits beforehand; these are the best and most functional homes in the surrounding area, because some of them were used in various capacities by the local sector CCR and her subordinates."

I raise my eyebrows, fascinated.

Ella never told me about this. She's clearly been hiding this project from me for days—which is both concerning and not. Part of me is relieved to finally understand the distance I've felt between us, while the other part of me wishes I'd been involved.

"So, yeah, we've reclaimed several dozen acres of unregulated territory here," she says. "All of which, up until a couple of weeks ago, were under military control. I figured that, as long as we need absolute security—which might be a while—we can't live like we're in prison. We're going to need to expand the Sanctuary, and give our people here a real, viable life.

"It's going to be a long road to recovery," Ella adds with a sigh. "The work is going to be brutal. The least I can do is give proper shelter, privacy, and amenities to those dedicating their lives to its reconstruction. I want to rebuild all the houses in this area first. Then I want to build schools, and a proper hospital. We can safeguard some of the original undeveloped land, turning it into parks. I'm hoping it'll one day become a private campus—a new capital—as we rebuild the world. And then, maybe one day when things are safer, we can let down our walls and reunite with the general public."

"Wow."

I detach from her a moment to look up and down the street, then into the distance. What she's describing is an enormous undertaking. I can't believe how much space they were already able to reclaim. "This is a remarkable idea, Ella. Truly. It's brilliant." I look back at her, forcing a smile. "I only wish I could've helped."

"I really, really wanted to tell you about it," she says, her brows knitting together. "But I couldn't say anything because I knew you'd want to come see the area, and then you would've noticed all the building materials, and then you would've wanted to know why so many people were working so hard on this one house, and then you would've wanted to know who was going to live in it—"

"I wouldn't have asked that many questions."

She shoots me a hard look.

"No, you're right." I nod. "I would've ruined the surprise."

"HEY!"

I spin around at the sound of the familiar voice. Kenji is coming around the side yard of the house. He's holding a folding chair in one hand, and waving what appears to be a sprig of some kind of flower in the other. "You two coming in or what? Brendan is complaining about losing the light or some shit—he says the sun will be directly overhead in a couple of hours, which is apparently really bad for photos? Anyway, Nazeera is getting impatient, too; she says J needs to start getting ready soon."

143

I stare at Kenji, then Ella, dumbfounded. She already looks perfect. "Get ready how?"

"I have to put on my dress," she says, and laughs.

"And makeup," Kenji shouts from across the street. "Nazeera and Alia say they need to do her makeup. And something about her hair."

I stiffen. "You have a dress? But I thought—"

Ella kisses me on the cheek, cutting me off. "Okay, there might be a few more surprises left in the day."

"I'm not sure my heart can handle any more surprises, love."

"How's this for a surprise?" Kenji says, leaning against the folding chair. "This beautiful piece of shit right here?" He gestures at the dilapidated house next door. "This one's mine."

That wipes the smile off my face.

"That's right, buddy." Kenji is grinning now. "We're going to be neighbors."

TWELVE

Ella is soon whisked away by a tornado of women—Nazeera, Alia, and Lily—who come charging out the door in a swarm, enveloping her in their depths before I've even had a chance to say a proper goodbye.

There's little more than a faint squeak from Ella—

And she's gone.

I find myself standing alone in front of what I'm still processing as *my own home*, my mind spinning, heart racing, when Kenji walks over to me.

"C'mon, man," he says, still smiling. "You've got stuff to do, too."

I look at him. "What kind of stuff?"

"Well, first of all, this is for you," he says, offering me the small sprig I noticed in his hand earlier. "It's for your lapel. It's like a, you know—like a—a—"

"I know what a boutonniere is," I say stiffly. I accept the small spray, examining it now with surprise. It's a single gardenia nestled against a tasteful arrangement of its own glossy leaves, the stems tied up with a bit of black ribbon, struck through with a pin. The bundle is elegant and shockingly fragrant. Gardenias are in fact one of my favorite flowers.

I look up at Kenji then, unable to hide my confusion.

He shrugs. "Don't look at me, bro. I have no idea what kind of flower that is. J just told me what she wanted."

"Wait." I frown at that, more confused by the moment. "*You* did this?"

"I just did what she asked me to do, okay?" he says, putting up his hands. "So if you hate the flower you should talk to your fiancée, because it's not my fault—"

"But where did this flower come from? I saw people with flowers earlier, too, and I didn't understand where—"

"Oh." Kenji drops his hands. He stares at me a moment before saying, "The old sector headquarters. You remember how you guys always had these rare flower arrangements at 45? We never knew where or how they were being sourced, but everyone always thought it was strange that the HQ could get fancy orchids or whatever, while civilians couldn't get their hands on much more than dandelions. Anyway it was Juliette's idea, actually. She recommended we track down the flower guy who used to carry out orders for The Reestablishment in this area. He helped us get everything we needed—but the flowers weren't delivered until late last night. Another reason why J wanted to postpone."

"Right." I'm stunned. "Of course."

My astonishment has nothing to do with discovering that Ella is just as impressive and resourceful as I've always known her to be; no, I'm simply incapable of believing anyone would go to such lengths for *me*.

I'm still reeling a bit as I attempt to pin the flower to my sweater, when Kenji holds up a hand again.

"Uh, don't do that just yet," he says. "Come on."

"Why?"

"Because, man, we still have things to do."

He turns as if to go, but I remain rooted to the ground.

"What kinds of things?" I ask.

"You know." He makes an indecipherable gesture, frowning at me. "Wedding things?"

I feel myself tense. "If the purpose of my question has not yet been made evident to you, Kishimoto, allow me to be crystal clear now: I am asking you to be specific."

He laughs at that. "Do you ever do anything anyone asks you to do without first asking a million questions?"

"No."

"Right." He laughs again. "Okay. Well, J is probably going to be getting her hair and makeup done for a little while, which means you can help us finish setting up in the backyard. But first, Winston has a surprise for you."

"No, thank you."

Kenji blinks. "What do you mean, *no, thank you*?"

"I don't want any more surprises," I say, my chest constricting at the very thought. "I can't take any more surprises."

"Listen, I can honestly understand what you might be feeling right now." He sighs. "Your head is probably spinning. I tried to tell her—I told her it wasn't a good idea to spring a wedding on a person, but whatever. She just does her own thing. Anyway, this is a good surprise, I promise.

Plus, I can give you a little tour of your new place."

It's this last line that uproots me from where I stand.

There's a short set of steps leading up to the house, and I take them slowly, my heart pounding nervously as I look around. There's a sizable front porch with freshly painted beams and railings, a decent area to set up a table and chairs when the weather's nice. The large windows flanking the front door are accented with what appear to be functioning, pale-sage-green shutters, the front door painted to match. Slowly, I push open this door—which has been left ajar—crossing the threshold now with even greater trepidation. The wood floor underfoot creaks as I step into the front hall, the clamor and commotion of the room coming to a sudden, eerie halt as I enter.

Everyone turns to look at me.

The drumbeat in my chest pounds harder, and I feel, for a moment, afloat in this sea of uncertainty. I'm lost for words, having never been prepared, in all my life, to deal with such a strange scenario.

I try to think, then, of what Ella would do.

"Thank you," I say into the silence. "For everything."

The crowd erupts into whoops and cheers at that, the tension gone in an instant. People shout congratulations into the din, and as my nerves begin to relax, I'm better able to make out their individual faces—some I recognize; others I don't. Adam is the first to wave at me from a distant corner, and I notice then that he's got his free arm wrapped around the waist of a young woman with blond hair.

Alia.

I remember her name. She's a painfully quiet girl, one of the troupe who collected Ella earlier—and one of Winston's friends. Today she seems unusually bright and happy.

So does Adam.

I nod at him in response, and he smiles before turning away to whisper something in Alia's ear. James appears then, almost out of nowhere, tapping Adam on the arm aggressively, after which the three of them engage in a brief, quiet discussion that ends with Alia nodding fervently. She kisses Adam on the cheek before disappearing into a room just down the hall, and I stare at the door of this room long after she's closed it.

Ella must be in there.

For what feels like a dangerously long time I feel paralyzed in place, studying the imperfect walls and windows of a home that is mine, that will be mine today, tonight, tomorrow.

I can't believe it.

I could kiss its rotting floor.

"Follow me," Kenji says, his voice stirring me from my stupor. He leads me through the small house as if he's walked these paths a hundred times—and I realize then that he has.

All these days he's been working on this project. For Ella. For me.

I experience a sharp, distracting stab of guilt.

"Hello?" Kenji waves a hand in front of my face. "You

want to see the kitchen, or no? I mean, I don't really recommend it, because the kitchen probably needs the most work, but hey, it's your house."

"I don't need to see the kitchen."

"Great, then we'll just get right to it. Winston first, then the backyard. Sound good? You never seem to have a problem working in a suit, so I don't think it'll be a problem for you today, either."

I sigh. "I have no problem assisting with manual labor, Kishimoto. In fact, I would've been happy to do so earlier."

"Great, well, that's what we like to hear." Kenji slaps me on the back, and I grit my teeth to keep from killing him.

"All right," he says. "So, I'm not going to torture you with any more unknowns, because I don't think you actually like surprises. I also think you're probably the kind of guy who likes to be able to pre-visualize stuff—helps manage the anxiety of not knowing things—so I'm going to walk you through this step-by-step. Sound good?"

I come to a sudden stop, staring at Kenji like I've never seen him before. "What?"

"What do you mean, *what*?"

"How did you know that I don't like surprises?"

"Bro, you're forgetting that I watched you have an actual panic attack." He taps his head. "I know some things, okay?"

I narrow my eyes at him.

"Okay, well"—he clears his throat—"there's also this doctor we're working with now—one of the ladies leading the exit evaluations for the asylum residents—and she's, like, crazy smart. She's got all kinds of interesting things to say about these patients, and everything they've been through. Anyway, you should talk to her. We had a patient who was cleared—healthy, fine, totally normal—to be returned to their relatives, but this dude couldn't get on a plane without having a major panic attack. The doctor was explaining to Sam that, for some people, getting on a plane is terrifying because they have to be able to trust the pilot to control the plane—and some people just can't trust like that. They can't cede control. Anyway, it made me think of you."

I deeply loathe this comparison, and I tell him as much. "I am perfectly capable of getting on planes," I point out.

"Yeah, I know, but—you know what I mean, right? Generally?"

"No."

Kenji sighs. "I'm just saying that I think it probably helps you to know exactly what's going to happen next. You like being in control. You don't like not knowing things. You probably like to imagine things in your head before they happen."

"You had a single conversation with a doctor and now you think you're capable of psychoanalyzing me?"

"I'm not—" Kenji throws up his arms. "You know what, whatever. Let's go. Winston's waiting."

"Wait."

Kenji looks up at me, irritation written all over his features. "What?"

"There might be a small grain of truth in what you said. A very, very small grain."

"*I knew it*," he says, pointing at me. "I told her, too, I was like, wow, you should really talk to this one guy we know, he could use a lot of help working through some—"

"You didn't." A muscle jumps in my jaw. "Tell me you didn't actually say that to her."

"I did too say that to her. She was a smart lady, and I think she might have some really interesting things to say to you. She was talking about some of these inmates and the problems they were facing and I was like, oh my God, you could be describing Warner right now."

"I see," I say, and nod. "I should just kill you here, shouldn't I? In my own house. On my wedding day. It could be your gift to me."

"*This*, right here!" He throws out his arms. "This is a perfect example! You don't know how to problem solve without resorting to murder! How do you not see this as an issue?" He shakes his head. "I don't know, man, you really might want to consider—"

I take a sharp breath, staring up at the ceiling. "For the love of God, Kishimoto. Where is Winston, and what does he want with me?"

"Did someone say my name?" Winston pops his head out of a door in the corridor ahead. "Come on in. I'm all ready for you."

I shoot Kenji a scathing look before retreating down the hall, peering into the new room with some concern. It appears to be some kind of a bedroom, though it's in desperate need of work. And paint. Winston has set up what appears to be a small command center—a dingy folding table displaying an artfully arranged selection of ties, bow ties, cuff links, and socks. I stare at it, beginning to understand, but I'm distracted by a strange, pungent odor that only seems to strengthen the longer I stand here.

"What on earth is that smell?" I ask, frowning at the old wood paneling.

"Yeah," Winston says, shrugging. "We don't know. We think maybe there's a dead rat in the wall. Or maybe a couple of dead rats."

"What?" I look at him sharply.

"Or!" Kenji says brightly. "Or, it's just mold!"

"A delightful alternative."

"Okay." Winston claps his hands together, beaming. "We can talk about the rats tomorrow. You ready to see your suit?"

"What suit?"

"Your wedding suit," Winston says, staring at me now with a strange expression on his face. "You didn't really think you were getting married today in the clothes you're wearing, did you?"

"Not they aren't nice clothes," Kenji adds. "To be fair."

I meet Winston's eyes. "I haven't been able to predict a single thing that was going to happen to me today. How was I supposed to know that you'd managed to salvage my wedding suit from the wreckage? No one told me."

153

"We didn't salvage it from the wreckage," Winston says, laughing. "I made you a new one."

This leaves me briefly speechless. I stare at Winston, then Kenji. "You made me a new suit? How? Why? *When?*"

"What do you mean?" Winston is still smiling. "We couldn't let you get married without a proper suit."

"But how did you find the time? You must've—"

"Been up all night?" Brendan ducks his head into the room, then steps fully inside. "Finishing most of the work by hand? Yes, Winston was up all night on your behalf. Hardly slept at all. Which is why it wasn't very nice of you to be so rude to him this morning."

I glance from Brendan to Winston to Kenji.

I have no idea what to say, and I'm just thinking of how to respond when Adam and James show up at the door, two sets of knuckles knocking a rapid staccato on the frame.

"Hi!" James says, abandoning the door and his brother to invade my personal space. "Did they tell you I'm the only kid allowed at the wedding?"

"No."

"Well, I am. I'm the only kid allowed at the wedding. My friends are super jealous right now because they're all stuck in class."

"And was there any particular reason," I ask carefully, "why they made an exception for you?"

James rolls his eyes and lunges at me, hugging me right around the middle in a show of unprecedented self-assurance that shocks me, briefly, into paralysis.

"Congratulations," he says against my sweater. "I'm really happy for you guys."

I have to remind myself that James is not only—biologically—my brother, but also a child, and undeserving of rejection. I pat him on the head in a single, wooden movement that startles a laugh out of Kenji, a gasp from Winston, stunned silence from Brendan, and slack-jawed astonishment from Adam.

I clear my throat, disengaging from James as gently as I can.

"Thank you," I say to him.

"You're welcome," he says, beaming. "Thanks for inviting me."

"I didn't invi—"

"So!" Adam cuts me off, trying and failing now to fight a smile. "We, um, we just came by to check in with you on a couple of details." He glances at James. "Right, buddy?"

James nods. "Right."

"First of all: Did anyone talk to you about your vows? Do you want to go traditional, or do you plan on saying something—"

"He's going traditional," Kenji says, answering for me before I've had a chance to respond. "I already told Castle." He turns to face me. "Castle is doing the ceremony, by the way—you know that, right?"

"No," I say, staring at him. "I did not know that. But what makes you think I don't want to write my own vows?"

He shrugs. "You don't strike me as the kind of guy who

likes to get up in front of a crowd and shoot from the heart. But I'm happy to be wrong," he says. "If you want to write your own vows, stand in front of a ton of people—most of whom you hardly know—and tell Juliette her face reminds you of a sunrise, no problem. Castle is flexible."

"I would rather impale myself on a pike."

"Yeah." Kenji grins. "That's what I thought."

Kenji turns away to ask Adam a question, something about ceremony logistics, and I study the back of his head, confused.

How? I want to ask. *How did you know?*

Winston unfolds a garment bag, hangs it on a nearby door, and unzips the length of it while Brendan unearths a box of shoes from a dingy closet.

Adam says, "Okay, I still have a few questions for Warner, but I need to confirm with Castle about the vows, so we'll be right back—and I'll find out about the music—"

And I feel as if I've stepped into a strange, alternate reality, into a world where I didn't think I'd ever belong. I could never have anticipated that somehow, somewhere along this tumultuous path—

I'd acquired friends.

THIRTEEN

The backyard is a modest rectangle of scorched land, the sparse and parched grass nicely obscured by a selection of time-worn wooden folding chairs, the arrangement parted down the middle by an artificial aisle, all of which face a hand-wrought wedding arch. Two thick, ten-foot cylindrical wooden stakes have been hammered into the ground, the five feet of empty space between them bridged at the top by a raw, severed tree limb, the joints bound together by rope. This crudely constructed bower is decorated with a robust selection of colorful wildflowers; leaves and petals flutter in the gentle breeze, infusing the early-morning air with their combined fragrance.

The scene is at once simple and breathtaking, and I am immobilized by the sight of it.

I am in a perfectly tailored, dark green, three-piece suit with a white shirt and black tie. My original suit was black, by request; Winston told me he decided to go with this deep shade of green because he thought it would suit my eyes and offset my gold hair. I wanted to argue with him except that I was genuinely impressed with the quality of his work, and did not protest when he handed me a pair of black, patent leather shoes to match. Absently, I touch the gardenia affixed to my lapel, feeling the always-present weight of the velvet box against my thigh.

There are folding tables arranged along the opposite end of the yard still waiting for their tablecloths, and I have been assigned the task of dressing them. I have also been ordered to see to the tables and chairs that need to be arranged inside the as-yet-unfurnished living and dining rooms, where the reception is meant to take place later this evening after a break post-ceremony, during which our guests will change work shifts, see to things back at the base, and Ella and I will have a chance to take pictures.

This all sounds so perfectly human as to render me ill.

I have, as a result, done none of things requested of me. I've been unable to move from this spot, staring at the wedding arch where I will soon be expected to stand and wait.

I clutch the back of a chair, holding on for dear life as the weight of the day's revelations inhale me, drowning me in their depths. Kenji is right; I don't enjoy surprises. This is fundamentally true, and yet—I would like to be the kind of person who enjoys surprises. I want to live a life like this, to be able to withstand unexpected moments of kindness delivered by the person I love most in the world. It's only that I don't know what to do with these experiences; my body doesn't know how to accept or digest them.

I am so happy it's physically uncomfortable; I am so full of hope it seems to depress my chest, forcing the air from my lungs.

I draw in a sharp breath against this feeling, forcing

158

myself to be calm while doing, over and over, the mental gymnastics necessary to remind myself that my fears are irrational, when I feel the approach of a familiar nervous energy.

I turn around carefully to meet her, surprised she's sought me out at all.

"Hey," Sam says, trying to smile. She's dressed up; she even appears to have attempted something like makeup, her eyelids shimmering in the soft light of the morning. "Big day."

"Yes."

"Listen, I'm sorry." She sighs. "I didn't mean to lash out at you like that last night. Really, I didn't."

I nod, then look away, staring into the distance. This yard is separated from its neighbor's by only a short, shabby wooden fence. Kenji will no doubt spend the rest of our lives tormenting me from over top of it.

Sam sighs again, louder this time. "I know you and I don't always see eye to eye," she says, "but I'm hoping maybe—if we get to know each other better—that'll change."

I look up at that, analyzing Sam now.

She is being sincere, but I find her suggestion unlikely. I notice Nouria in my periphery then, huddled up with her father and three others, and shift my gaze in her direction. She's wearing a simple sheath dress in a shade of chartreuse that compliments her dark skin. She appears to be happy at the moment—smiling—which even I realize is rare for Nouria these days.

Sam follows my line of sight, seeming to understand where my thoughts have gone. "I know she's a little hard on you sometimes, but she's been under crazy amounts of pressure lately. She's never had to oversee so many people, or so many details, and The Reestablishment has been a lot harder to deconstruct than we'd thought—you can't even imagine—"

"Can't I?" I almost smile, even as my jaw tenses. "You think me incapable of understanding the weight of the burden we shoulder now?"

Sam looks away. "I didn't say that. That's not what I meant."

"Our position is worse than precarious," I say to her. "And whatever you think of me—whatever you think you understand about me—I am only trying to help."

For the third time, Sam sighs.

Now, more than ever, those of us at the Sanctuary should be allied, but Sam and Nouria have grown to detest me over the last couple of weeks because I challenge them at every turn, refusing to agree with their tactics or ideology when I find it lacking—and unwilling to acquiesce merely to get along.

They find this fundamentally infuriating, and I don't care.

I refuse to do anything that would put Ella's life in jeopardy, and letting our movement fail would be doing exactly that.

"I want us to try again," Sam says, steely now as she

meets my eyes. "I want us to start over. We've been fighting a lot lately, and I think you would agree with me that it's not sustainable. We should be united right now."

"United? Nouria deliberately made me think I couldn't get married. She willfully manipulated the truth to make the situation seem dire, simply to wound me. How can such petty machinations form any foundation for unity?"

"She wasn't trying to wound you. She was trying to protect you."

"In what alternate reality could that possibly be true?"

Sam's anger flares. "You know what your problem is?"

"Yes. The list is long."

"*Oh my God,*" she says, her irritation building. "This, *this* is exactly your problem. You think you know everything. You're uncooperative, you're uncompromising, and you've already decided you've figured everything out. You don't know how to be part of a *team*—"

"You and Nouria don't know how to take constructive criticism."

"Constructive criticism?" Sam gapes at me. "You call your criticism *constructive*?"

"You're free to call it whatever you like," I say unkindly. "But I refuse to remain silent when I believe you and Nouria are making the wrong choices. You regularly forget that I was raised within The Reestablishment, from its infancy, and that there is a great deal I understand about the mechanics of our enemies' minds—more than you are even willing to consider—"

"All okay over here?" Castle asks, striding toward us. His smile is uncertain. "We're not talking about work right now, are we?"

"Oh, everything is fine," Sam says too brightly. "I was just reminding Warner here how much Nouria has done to keep him and Juliette safe on their wedding day. An event I think we all agree would render them both most vulnerable to an outside threat."

I go suddenly still.

"Well—yes," Castle says, confused. "Of course. You already know that, though, don't you, Mr. Warner? News of your impending nuptials was beginning to spread, and we feared the possible repercussions for both you and Ms. Ferrars on such a joyous day."

I'm still staring at Sam when I say quietly: "That's why you all lied to me yesterday?"

"Nouria thought it was imperative that we convince *you*," Sam says stiffly, "more than anyone else, that you wouldn't be getting married today. The supreme kids knew about the wedding before they left, and Nouria worried that even a whiff of an exchange on the subject yesterday might be intercepted in your daily communications, which we wanted to make certain you carried out as normal. The notifications Juliette sent out last night were done in code."

"I see," I say, glancing again at Nouria, who's now deep in conversation with the girls—Sonya and Sara—both of whom are holding what appear to be small black suitcases.

I should be touched by this gesture of protection, but the

fact that they felt I couldn't be trusted with such a plan does little to improve my mood.

"You do realize you could've simply asked me to say nothing, don't you? I'm perfectly capable of discretion—"

"What is going on between you two?" Castle frowns. "This is not the energy I expected from either of you on—"

"Sir?" Ian is standing at the sliding screen door—the only access point into the house from the backyard—and motioning Castle forward with an agitated wave. "Can you come here, please? Now?"

Castle frowns, then glances between myself and Sam. "There will be plenty of time to discuss unpleasant matters later, do you understand? Today is a day of celebration. *For all of us.*"

"Oh, don't worry," Sam says to Castle. "Everything will be fine—right, Warner?"

"Perhaps," I say, holding her gaze.

Sam and I say nothing else, and Castle shakes his head before stalking off, leaving the two of us alone to enjoy an uncomfortable moment of silence.

Sam takes a sudden deep breath.

"Anyway," she says loudly, looking around now for an exit. "Exciting day. Best wishes and everything."

My jaw clenches. I'm saved the need to respond to this limp performance of civility by the abrupt, sharp bark of a dog, accompanied by the timid admonishment of a human.

Sam and I both spin around toward the sounds.

An animal I hardly recognize is scratching wildly at the

screen door, yapping—at me, specifically—from several feet away. Its once mangy, matted fur is now a healthy brown, with an unexpected smattering of white; this accomplishment is undermined by its bright red collar and ridiculous, matching headband, the undignified accessory crowned with a large crimson bow, which sits atop the animal's head. The perpetrator of this crime is standing just beyond the dog, a tall, redheaded young woman desperately begging the pup to be calm.

Kenji had said her name was Yara.

She struggles in vain; the creature pays her no mind as he barks over and over, all the while pawing anxiously at the screen door—*my screen door*—which he will no doubt destroy if he does not soon desist.

"Let him out," I say to her, my voice carrying.

The young woman startles at that, quickly fumbling now to unlatch the screen door. When she finally manages to slide the panel open, the animal all but lunges through the doorway, yanking her along with him.

Beside me, Sam makes a poorly muffled sound of disgust.

"I didn't realize you hated animals," I say without looking at her.

"Oh, I love animals. Animals are better at being human than people are."

"I don't disagree."

"Shocking."

I turn to face her, surprised. "Why are you so angry?"

Sam sighs and nods discreetly at Yara, who waves enthusiastically even as she's dragged along in our direction.

I raise my eyebrows at Sam.

"Oh, don't look at me like that," she says, irritated. "You have no idea what Nouria and I have had to deal with since you arrived. It got a hundred times worse after everyone decided you were some kind of a hero. It was a really low moment for us, realizing that so many people we respected were shockingly shallow."

"If it makes you feel any better," I say, taking a breath as I lift a hand in Yara's direction, "I don't like it, either."

"Bullshit," Sam says automatically, but I sense her flicker of uncertainty.

I lower my voice as Yara closes in on us. "Would you enjoy being reduced to nothing but your physical footprint, forced all the while to absorb the weight of strangers' indecent emotions as they assess and undress you?"

Sam stiffens beside me. She turns to look at me, her feelings scattered and confused. I feel her reexamining me.

"Hi!" Yara says, coming to a stop in front of us.

She is an objectively kind young woman; I recognize this even as I fight back a wave of revulsion. Yara has done the animal—and me, by extension—a great courtesy, which she needn't have done for a stranger on such short notice. Still, her feelings are both generous and disconcerting, some of them loud enough to make me physically uncomfortable.

The dog is wise enough to halt at my feet.

He lifts a tentative paw as if to touch me, and I give him

a sharp look, after which the paw retreats. In the interven- ing silence, the dog stares up at me with big, dark eyes, his tail wagging furiously.

"It was kind of you to wash the animal," I say to Yara, still staring at the dog. "He looks much better now."

"Oh, it was my pleasure," she says, hesitating before add- ing: "You look—you look really, really nice today."

My smile is tight.

I don't want to feel what she's feeling right now. I don't want to know these things—not ever—but especially not on my wedding day.

I bend down to look the dog in the eye and draw a gentle hand over his head, into which he eagerly leans. He sniffs me, nosing the palm of my hand, and I pull away before the beast decides to lick me. I decide instead to check his collar; there is a single metal coin hanging from the red strap, and I pinch it between two fingers, the better to examine it.

It reads: DOG.

"That's what you said you wanted to call him, right?" Yara is still smiling. "*Dog?*"

I look up at her then, meeting the young woman's eyes against my better judgment, and her smile trembles.

Sam stifles a laugh.

"Yes," I say slowly. "I suppose I did say something like that."

Yara beams. "Well, he's all yours now. Happy wedding and everything."

I stand up sharply. "What?"

"Oh, and it looks like he's already been neutered, so I think he's had a family before. You made a great choice. I'm not sure what kind of dog he is—he's definitely some kind of mixed breed—but he's not totally wild, and I think he'll be a good—

"I'm afraid you've gravely misunderstood the situation. I don't want a dog. I merely wanted you to wash the animal, and maybe feed it—"

Sam is laughing openly now, and I pivot to face her.

"You think this is funny? What am I supposed to do with a dog?"

"Um, I don't know"—she shoots me an incredulous look—"give it a loving home?"

"Don't be ridiculous."

"I'm—I'm so sorry," Yara says, her eyes widening now with panic. "I thought he was *your* dog—I didn't think he was— I mean he doesn't obey anyone else, and he seems really attached to you—"

"Don't worry, Yara," Sam says gently. "You did great. Warner just wasn't expecting you to be so generous, and he's kind of, um, overwhelmed with gratitude right now. Isn't that right, Warner?" She turns to me. "Yara was so kind to get . . . *Dog* here all washed and ready for your wedding day. Wasn't she?"

"Very kind," I say, my jaw tensing.

Yara looks nervously in my direction. "Really?"

Briefly, I meet her eyes. "Really."

She flushes.

"Yara, why don't you hold on to"—she fights back a smile—"*Dog* until the end of the ceremony? Maybe make sure he gets something to eat."

"Oh, sure." Yara shoots me one last furtive look before tugging gently on the animal's leash. The dog whines at that, then barks as she coaxes him, one foot at a time, back toward the house.

I turn my eyes skyward. "This is unforgivable."

"Why?" I can hear practically hear Sam smile. "I bet Juliette would love to have a dog."

I look at Sam. "Did you know, I once watched a dog vomit—and then proceed to *eat* its own vomit."

"Okay, but—"

"And then vomit. Again."

Sam crosses her arms. "That was one dog."

"Another dog once defecated right in front of me while I was patrolling a compound."

"That's perfectly norm—"

"After which it promptly ate its own feces."

Sam crosses her arms. "All right. Well. That's still better than the awful things I've seen humans do."

I'm prevented from responding by a sudden swell of commotion. People are starting to rush around, pushing past us to scatter wildflowers in the grassy aisle. Sonya and Sara, clad in identical green gowns, take positions adjacent to the wedding arch, their black suitcases gone. In their hands they hold matching violins and bows, the sight of which paralyzes me anew. I feel that familiar pain in my chest, something like fear.

It's beginning.

"You're right, though," I say quietly to Sam, wondering, for the hundredth time, what Ella might be doing inside the house. "She'd love to have a dog."

"Wait— I'm sorry, did you just say I was *right* about something?"

I release a sharp breath. It sounds almost like a laugh.

"You know," Sam says thoughtfully. "I think this might be the most pleasant conversation you and I have ever had."

"Your standards are very low, then."

"When it comes to you, Warner, my standards have to be low."

I manage to smile at that, but I'm still distracted. Castle is walking toward the arch now, a small leather-bound note-book in his hand, a sprig of lavender pinned to his lapel. He nods at me as he goes, and I can only stare, feeling suddenly like I can't breathe.

"I've seen her, by the way," Sam says softly.

I turn to face her.

"Juliette." Sam smiles. "She looks beautiful."

I'm struggling to formulate a response to this when I sense the approach of a familiar presence; his hand lands on my arm, and for the first time, I don't flinch.

"Hey, man," Kenji says, materializing at my side in a surprisingly sharp suit. "You ready? There's not much of a wedding party, so we're not doing a processional, which means J will be walking down the aisle pretty soon. Nazeera

169

just gave us the ten-minute . . ."

Kenji trails off, distracted as if on cue, by Nazeera herself. She saunters toward the wedding arch, tall and steady in a gauzy, blush-colored gown. She grins at Castle, who acknowledges her with a smile of his own; Nazeera takes a position just off to the side of the arch, adjusting her skirts as she settles in place.

It becomes terrifyingly clear to me then exactly where Ella is expected to soon stand. Where *I* am expected to soon stand.

"But I haven't finished with the tablecloths," I say, "or the seating inside—"

"Yeah. I noticed." Kenji takes a sharp breath, tearing his gaze away from Nazeera to look me in the eye. "Anyway, don't worry. We took care of it. You seemed really busy standing still for half an hour, staring at nothing. We didn't want to interrupt."

"All right, I think I should get going," Sam says, offering me a real, genuine smile. "Nouria is saving me a seat. Good luck out there."

I nod at her as she goes, surprised to discover that, despite the long road ahead, there might be hope of a truce between us after all.

"Okay." Kenji claps his hands together. "First things first: do you need to go to the bathroom or anything before we start? Personally, I think you should go even if you don't think you have to, because it would be really awkward if you suddenly had t—"

"Stop."

"Oh—right!" Kenji says, slapping his hand to his forehead. "My bad, bro, I forgot—you never have to use the bathroom, do you?"

"No."

"No, of course not. Because that would be human, and we both know you're secretly a robot."

I sigh, resisting the urge to run my hands through my hair.

"Seriously, though—anything you need to do before you go up there? You've got the ring, right?"

"No." My heart is pounding furiously in my chest now. "And yes."

"Okay, then." Kenji nods toward the wedding arch. "Go ahead and get into position under that flower thing. Castle will show you exactly where to stand—"

I turn sharply to face him. "You're not coming with me?"

Kenji goes stock-still at that, his mouth slightly agape. I realize, a moment too late, exactly what I've just suggested— and still I can't bring myself to retract the question, and I can't explain why.

Right now, it doesn't seem to matter.

Right now, I can't quite feel my legs.

Kenji, to his credit, does not laugh in my face. Instead, his expression relaxes by micrometers, his dark eyes assessing me in that careful way I detest.

"Yeah," he says finally. "Of course I'm coming with you."

FOURTEEN

Sunlight glances off my eyes, the glare shifting, flickering through a webbing of bare branches as a gentle breeze moves through the yard, fluttering leaves and skirts and flower petals. The scent of the gardenia affixed to my lapel wafts upward, filling my head with a heady perfume as the sharp collar of my shirt scrapes against my neck, my tie too tight; I clasp my hands in front of me to keep from adjusting it, my palms brushing against the wool of my suit, the fabric soft and lightweight and still somehow abrasive, suffocating me as I stand here in stiff shoes sinking slowly into dead grass, staring out at a sea of people come to bear witness to what might be one of the most publicly vulnerable moments of my life.

I can't seem to breathe.

I can't seem to make out their faces, but I can feel them, the individual emotional capsules that make up the members of this audience, the collective frenzy of their thoughts and feelings overwhelming me in a breathtaking crush that crowds my already chaotic thoughts. I feel myself begin to panic—my heart rate increasing rapidly—as I try to digest this noise, to tune out the barrage of other people's nervousness and excitement. It's a struggle even to hear myself think, to unearth my own consciousness. I try, desperately, to find an anchor in this madness.

It is nearly impossible.

Sonya and Sara lift their violins, sharing a glance before one of the sisters, Sonya, takes the lead, launching into the opening of Pachelbel's Canon in D. Sara soon accompanies her, and the evocative, heart-wrenching notes fill the air, igniting in my chest a flare of emotion that only intensifies my apprehension, pulling my nerves taut to a painful degree. I swallow, hard, my pulse racing dangerously fast. My hands seem to spark and fade with feeling, prickling hot and cold, and I flex them into fists.

"Hey, man," Kenji whispers beside me. "You all right?"

I shake my head an inch.

"What's wrong?"

I can feel Kenji studying my face.

"Oh—*shit*—are you having a panic attack?"

"Not yet," I manage to say. I close my eyes, try to breathe. "It's too loud in here."

"The music?"

"*The people.*"

"Okay. Okay. Shit. So you can, like, feel everything they're feeling right now? Right. *Shit.* Of course you can. Okay. All right, what should I do? You want me to talk to you? How about I just talk to you? Why don't you just focus on me, on the sound of my voice. Fade everything else out."

"I don't know if that will work," I say, taking a shaky breath. "But I can try."

"Cool. Okay. First of all, open your eyes. Juliette is going to walk out in a couple of minutes, and you won't want to miss it. Her dress is awesome." He whispers this, his voice altered just enough that I can tell he's trying not to move his lips. "I'm not supposed to tell you anything about it, because, you know, it's supposed to be a surprise, but whatever, we're throwing surprises out the window right now because this is an emergency, and I have a feeling that once you see her your brain will do that creepy super-focus thing it always does—you know, like when you ignore literally everyone around you—and then you'll start feeling better because, um, yeah"—he laughs, nervously—"you know what? I'm beginning to realize only right this second that, uh, when she's around you don't even seem to notice other people, so, um—until then I can—yeah, I'm just going to describe her to you, because, like I said, she's going to look great. Her dress is, like, really, really pretty, and I don't even know anything about dresses, so that should tell you something."

The sound of his voice is a strange lifeline.

The more he speaks, filling my head with easily digestible nonsense, I feel my heart rate start to slow, the iron fist around my lungs beginning, slowly, to unclench.

I force my eyes open, and the scene briefly blurs in and out of focus, the pounding of my heart still loud in my head. I glance at Kenji, who is staring straight ahead, his face at rest as if nothing is amiss. This helps ground me, somehow, and I manage to pull myself together long enough to look down the petal-dusted aisle.

"So Juliette's dress is, um, like, really glittery, but also really soft-looking? Winston and Alia had to come up with a new design on such short notice," Kenji explains, "but they were able to repurpose some gown you guys got at the Supply Center yesterday. There was lots of, like, sheer fluffy fabric, I don't know what it's call—"

"Tulle."

"Yes. Tulle. Yes. Whatever. Anyway Alia spent all night, like, first of all, making it nicer, and then sewing these little glittery beads all over it—but, like, in a nice way. It's really nice. And it's got, like, these little tulle sleeves that aren't really sleeves—they sort of fall off the shoulder— Hey, is this helping?"

"Yes," I say, drawing in a full breath for the first time in minutes.

"Great, so—nice sleeves, and, and um, you know, it's got a long fluffy skirt— Okay, yeah, I'm sorry, bro, but I'm kind of out of descriptions for Juliette's dress, but— Oh, hey, here's a fun fact: Did you know that Sonya and Sara used to be, like, young virtuosos, way back in the day, pre-Reestablishment?"

"No."

"Yeah—yeah, so they started playing violin when they were fresh out of diapers. Pretty cool, huh? Nazeera helped us confiscate the violins they're using today from old

175

Reestablishment holdings. They're playing this song from *memory*. I don't know what it's called, but I'm pretty sure it's something fancy, from some old dead dude—"

"Of course you know what it's called," I say, still staring straight ahead. "Everyone knows it."

"Well *I* don't know it."

"This is the work of German composer Johann Pachelbel," I explain, struggling not to frown. "It's often called Pachelbel's Canon in D, because it was meant to be played in the key of D major. Do you know nothing about music?"

"Yeah, I don't even know what the hell you just said."

"How can y—"

"All right, shut up, no one cares—the music is changing, do you hear that? When it goes high like that? That means she's going to come out any second now—"

The audience rises almost at once, a rush of breaths and bodies clambering to their feet, craning their necks, and for a moment, I can't see her at all.

And then, suddenly, I do.

Relief hits me like a gust, leaving me so suddenly unsteady I worry, for a moment, that I might not make it.

Ella looks spun from gossamer, glowing as she glitters in the soft light. Her gown has a corseted, glimmering bodice that flows into a soft, decadent skirt, her arms bare save delicate, off-the-shoulder scraps of tulle that graze her skin.

She is luminous.

I've never seen her wear makeup, and I have no idea what they've done to her face, except that she is now so beautiful

176

as to be unreal, her hair in an elegant arrangement atop her head, a long veil gracing her shoulders, flowing with her as she walks.

She does not look like she belongs in this world, or in this dingy backyard, or in this dilapidated neighborhood, or on this crumbling planet. She is above it. Above us all. A spark of light separated from the sun.

A dangerous heat builds behind my eyes and I force myself to fight it back, to remain calm, but when she sees me, she smiles—and I nearly lose the fight.

"I told you it was a nice dress," Kenji whispers.

"Kenji."

"Yes?"

"Thank you," I say, still staring at Ella. "For everything."

"Anytime," he says, his voice more subdued than before. "This is the beginning of a new chapter for all of us, man. For the whole world. This wedding is making history right now. You know that, right? Nothing is ever going to be the same."

Ella glides toward me, nearly within reach. I feel my heart pounding in my chest, happiness threatening to destroy me. I'm smiling now, smiling like the most ordinary of men, staring at the most extraordinary woman I've ever known.

"Believe me," I whisper. "I do."

Keep reading for a sneak peek at

THIS WOVEN KINGDOM,

the first book in Tahereh Mafi's stunning fantasy series!

ONE

ALIZEH STITCHED IN THE KITCHEN by the light of star and fire, sitting, as she often did, curled up inside the hearth. Soot stained her skin and skirts in haphazard streaks: smudges along the crest of a cheek, a dusting of yet more darkness above one eye. She didn't seem to notice.

Alizeh was cold. No, she was *freezing*.

She often wished she were a body with hinges, that she might throw open a door in her chest and fill its cavity with coal, then kerosene. Strike a match.

Alas.

She tugged up her skirts and shifted nearer the fire, careful lest she destroy the garment she still owed the illegitimate daughter of the Lojjan ambassador. The intricate, glittering piece was her only order this month, but Alizeh nursed a secret hope that the gown would conjure clients on its own, for such fashionable commissions were, after all, the direct result of an envy born only in a ballroom, around a dinner table. So long as the kingdom remained at peace, the royal elite—legitimate and illegitimate alike— would continue to host parties and incur debt, which meant Alizeh might yet find ways to extract coin from their embroidered pockets.

She shivered violently then, nearly missing a stitch,

nearly toppling into the fire. As a toddling child Alizeh
had once been so desperately cold she'd crawled onto the
searing hearth on purpose. Of course it had never occurred
to her that she might be consumed by the blaze; she'd been
but a babe following an instinct to seek warmth. Alizeh
couldn't have known then the singularity of her affliction,
for so rare was the frost that grew inside her body that she
stood in stark relief even among her own people, who were
thought to be strange indeed.

A miracle, then, that the fire had only disintegrated
her clothes and clogged the small house with a smoke that
singed her eyes. A subsequent scream, however, signaled
to the snug tot that her scheme was at an end. Frustrated
by a body that would not warm, she'd wept frigid tears as
she was collected from the flames, her mother sustaining
terrible burns in the process, the scars of which Alizeh
would study for years to come.

"*Her eyes,*" the trembling woman had cried to her
husband, who'd come running at the sounds of distress.
"See what's happened to her eyes— They will kill her for
this—"

Alizeh rubbed her eyes now and coughed.

Surely she'd been too young to remember the precise
words her parents had spoken; no doubt Alizeh's was a
memory merely of a story oft-repeated, one so thoroughly
worn into her mind she only imagined she could recall her
mother's voice.

She swallowed.

Soot had stuck in her throat. Her fingers had gone

numb. Exhausted, she exhaled her worries into the hearth, the action disturbing to life another flurry of soot.

Alizeh coughed for the second time then, this time so hard she stabbed the stitching needle into her small finger. She absorbed the shock of pain with preternatural calm, carefully dislodging the bit before inspecting the injury.

The puncture was deep.

Slowly, almost one at a time, her fingers closed around the gown still clutched in her hand, the finest silk stanching the trickle of her blood. After a few moments—during which she stared blankly up, into the chimney, for the sixteenth time that night—she released the gown, cut the thread with her teeth, and tossed the gem-encrusted novelty onto a nearby chair.

Never fear; Alizeh knew her blood would not stain. Still, it was a good excuse to cede defeat, to set aside the gown. She appraised it now, sprawled as it was across the seat. The bodice had collapsed, bowing over the skirt much like a child might slump in a chair. Silk pooled around the wooden legs, beadwork catching the light. A weak breeze rattled a poorly latched window and a single candle blew out, taking with it the remaining composure of the commission. The gown slid farther down the chair, one heavy sleeve releasing itself with a hush, its glittering cuff grazing the sooty floor.

Alizeh sighed.

This gown, like all the others, was far from beautiful. She thought the design trite, the construction only passably good. She dreamed of unleashing her mind, of freeing her hands to create without hesitation—but the roar of Alizeh's imagination was quieted, always, by an unfortunate need for self-preservation.

It was only during her grandmother's lifetime that the Fire Accords had been established, unprecedented peace agreements that allowed Jinn and humans to mix freely for the first time in nearly a millennia. Though superficially identical, Jinn bodies had been forged from the essence of fire, imbuing in them certain physical advantages; while humans, whose beginnings were established in dirt and water, had long been labeled Clay. Jinn had conceded to the establishment of the Accords with a variegated relief, for the two races had been locked in bloodshed for eons, and though the enmity between them remained unresolved, all had tired of death.

The streets had been gilded with liquid sun to usher in the era of this tenuous peacetime, the empire's flag and coin reimagined in triumph. Every royal article was stamped with the maxim of a new age:

MERAS
May Equality Reign Always Supreme

Equality, as it turned out, had meant Jinn were to lower themselves to the weakness of humans, denying at all times the inherent powers of their race, the speed and strength and elective evanescence born unto their bodies. They were to cease at once what the king had declared "such supernatural operations" or face certain death, and Clay, who had exposed themselves as an insecure sort of creature, were only too willing to cry cheat no matter the context. Alizeh could still hear the screams, the riots in the streets—

She stared now at the mediocre gown.

Always she struggled not to design an article too exquisite, for extraordinary work came under harsher scrutiny, and was only too quickly denounced as the result of a preternatural trick.

Only once, having grown increasingly desperate to earn a decent living, had Alizeh thought to impress a customer not with style, but with craftsmanship. Not only was the quality of her work many orders of magnitude higher than that of the local modiste, but Alizeh could fashion an elegant morning gown in a quarter of the time, and had been willing to charge half as much.

The oversight had sent her to the gallows.

It had not been the happy customer, but the rival dressmaker who'd reported Alizeh to the magistrates. Miracle of miracles, she'd managed to evade their attempt to drag her away in the night, and fled the familiar countryside of her childhood for the anonymity of the city, hoping to be lost among the masses.

Would that she might slough off the burdens she carried with her always, but Alizeh knew an abundance of reasons to keep to the shadows, chief among them the reminder that her parents had forfeited their lives in the interest of her quiet survival, and to comport herself carelessly now would be to dishonor their efforts.

No, Alizeh had learned the hard way to relinquish her

commissions long before she grew to love them.

She stood and a cloud of soot stood with her, billowing around her skirts. She'd need to clean the kitchen hearth before Mrs. Amina came down in the morning or she'd likely be out on the street again. Despite her best efforts, Alizeh had been turned out onto the street more times than she could count. She'd always supposed it took little encouragement to dispose of that which was already seen as disposable, but these thoughts had done little to calm her.

Alizeh collected a broom, flinching a little as the fire died. It was late, very late. The steady *tick tick* of the clock wound something in her heart, made her anxious. Alizeh had a natural aversion to the dark, a rooted fear she could not fully articulate. She'd have rather worked a needle and thread by the light of the sun, but she spent her days doing the work that really mattered: scrubbing the rooms and latrines of Baz House, the grand estate of Her Grace, the Duchess Jamilah of Fetrous.

Alizeh had never met the duchess, only seen the glittering older woman from afar. Alizeh's meetings were with Mrs. Amina, the housekeeper, who'd hired Alizeh on a trial basis only, as she'd arrived with no references. As a result, Alizeh was not yet permitted to interact with the other servants, nor was she allotted a proper room in the servants' wing. Instead, she'd been given a rotting closet in the attic, wherein she'd discovered a cot, its moth-eaten mattress, and half a candle.

Alizeh had lain awake in her narrow bed that first night,

so overcome she could hardly breathe. She minded neither the rotting attic nor its moth-eaten mattress, for Alizeh knew herself to be in possession of great fortune. That any grand house was willing to employ a Jinn was shocking enough, but that she'd been given a room—a respite from the winter streets—

True, Alizeh had found stretches of work since her parents' deaths, and often she'd been granted leave to sleep indoors, or in the hayloft; but never had she been given a space of her own. This was the first time in years she had privacy, a door she might close; and Alizeh had felt so thoroughly saturated with happiness she feared she might sink through the floor. Her body shook as she stared up at the wooden beams that night, at the thicket of cobwebs that crowded her head. A large spider had unspooled a length of thread, lowering itself to look her in the eye, and Alizeh had only smiled, clutching a skin of water to her chest.

The water had been her single request.

"A skin of water?" Mrs. Amina had frowned at her, frowned as if she'd asked to eat the woman's child. "You can fetch your own water, girl."

"Forgive me, I would," Alizeh had said, eyes on her shoes, on the torn leather around the toe she'd not yet mended. "But I'm still new to the city, and I've found it difficult to access fresh water so far from home. There's no reliable cistern nearby, and I cannot yet afford the glass water in the market—"

Mrs. Amina roared with laughter.

Alizeh went silent, heat rising up her neck. She did not

know why the woman laughed at her.

"Can you read, child?"

Alizeh looked up without meaning to, registering the familiar, fearful gasp before she'd even locked eyes with the woman. Mrs. Amina stepped back, lost her smile.

"Yes," said Alizeh. "I can read."

"Then you must try to forget."

Alizeh started. "I beg your pardon?"

"Don't be daft." Mrs. Amina's eyes narrowed. "No one wants a servant who can read. You ruin your own prospects with that tongue. Where did you say you were from?"

Alizeh had frozen solid.

She couldn't tell whether this woman was being cruel or kind. It was the first time anyone had suggested her intelligence might present a problem to the position, and Alizeh wondered then whether it wasn't true: perhaps it *had* been her head, too full as it was, that kept landing her in the street. Perhaps, if she was careful, she might finally manage to keep a position for longer than a few weeks. No doubt she could feign stupidity in exchange for safety.

"I'm from the north, ma'am," she'd said quietly.

"Your accent isn't northern."

Alizeh nearly admitted aloud that she'd been raised in relative isolation, that she'd learned to speak as her tutors had taught her; but then she remembered herself, remembered her station, and said nothing.

"As I suspected," Mrs. Amina had said into the silence. "Rid yourself of that ridiculous accent. You sound like an idiot, pretending to be some kind of toff. Better yet, say nothing at all. If you can manage that, you may prove useful to me. I've heard your kind don't tire out so easily, and I expect your work to satisfy such rumors, else I'll not scruple to toss you back into the street. Have I made myself clear?"

"Yes, ma'am."

"You may have your skin of water."

"Thank you, ma'am." Alizeh curtsied, turned to go.

"Oh—and one more thing—"

Alizeh turned back. "Yes, ma'am?"

"Get yourself a snoda as soon as possible. I never want to see your face again."

TWO

"

ALIZEH HAD ONLY JUST PULLED open the door to her closet when she felt it, felt *him* as if she'd pushed her arms through the sleeves of a winter coat. She hesitated, heart pounding, and stood framed in the doorway.

Foolish.

Alizeh shook her head to clear it. She was imagining things, and no surprise: she was in desperate need of sleep. After sweeping the hearth, she'd had to scrub clean her sooty hands and face, too, and it had all taken much longer than she'd hoped; her weary mind could hardly be held responsible for its delirious thoughts at this hour.

With a sigh, Alizeh dipped a single foot into the inky depths of her room, feeling blindly for the match and candle she kept always near the door. Mrs. Amina had not allowed Alizeh a second taper to carry upstairs in the evenings, for she could neither fathom the indulgence nor the possibility that the girl might still be working long after the gas lamps had been extinguished. Even so, the housekeeper's lack of imagination did nothing to alter the facts as they were: this high up in so large an estate it was near impossible for distant light to penetrate. Save the occasional slant of the moon through a mingy corridor window, the attic presented opaque in the night; black as tar.

Were it not for the glimmer of the night sky to help her navigate the many flights to her closet, Alizeh might not have found her way, for she experienced a fear so paralyzing in the company of perfect darkness that, when faced with such a fate, she held an illogical preference for death.

Her single candle quickly found, the sought after match was promptly struck, a tear of air and the wick lit. A warm glow illuminated a sphere in the center of her room, and for the first time that day, Alizeh relaxed.

Quietly she pulled closed the closet door behind her, stepping fully into a room hardly big enough to hold her cot.

Just so, she loved it.

She'd scrubbed the filthy closet until her knuckles had bled, until her knees had throbbed. In these ancient, beautiful estates, most everything was once built to perfection, and buried under layers of mold, cobwebs, and caked-on grime, Alizeh had discovered elegant herringbone floors, solid wood beams in the ceiling. When she'd finished with it, the room positively gleamed.

Mrs. Amina had not, naturally, been to visit the old storage closet since it'd been handed over to the help, but Alizeh often wondered what the housekeeper might say if she saw the space now, for the room was unrecognizable. But then, Alizeh had long ago learned to be resourceful.

She removed her snoda, unwinding the delicate sheet of tulle from around her eyes. The silk was required of all those who worked in service, the mask marking its wearer as a member of the lower classes. The textile was designed for hard work, woven loosely enough to blur her features without obscuring necessary vision. Alizeh had chosen this profession with great forethought, and clung every day to the anonymity her position provided, rarely removing her snoda even outside of her room; for though most people did not understand the strangeness they saw in her eyes, she feared that one day the wrong person might.

She breathed deeply now, pressing the tips of her fingers against her cheeks and temples, gently massaging the face she'd not seen in what felt like years. Alizeh did not own a looking glass, and her occasional glances at the mirrors in Baz House revealed only the bottom third of her face: lips, chin, the column of her neck. She was otherwise a faceless servant, one of dozens, and had only vague memories of what she looked like—or what she'd once been told she looked like. It was the whisper of her mother's voice in her ear, the feel of her father's calloused hand against her cheek.

You are the finest of us all, he'd once said.

Alizeh closed her mind to the memory as she took off her shoes, set the boots in their corner. Over the years Alizeh had collected enough scraps from old commissions to stitch herself the quilt and matching pillow currently laid atop her mattress. Her clothes she hung from old nails wrapped meticulously in colorful thread; all other personal effects she'd arranged inside an apple crate she'd found discarded in one of the chicken coops.

She rolled off her stockings now and hung them—to air

them out—from a taut bit of twine. Her dress went to one of the colorful hooks, her corset to another, her snoda to the last. Everything Alizeh owned, everything she touched, was clean and orderly, for she had learned long ago that when a home was not found, it was forged; indeed it could be fashioned even from nothing.

Clad only in her shift, she yawned, yawned as she sat on her cot, as the mattress sank, as she pulled the pins from her hair. The day—and her long, heavy curls—crashed down around her shoulders.

Her thoughts had begun to slur.

With great reluctance she blew out the candle, pulled her legs against her chest, and fell over like a poorly weighted insect. The illogic of her phobia was consistent only in perplexing her, for when she was abed and her eyes closed, Alizeh imagined she could more easily conquer the dark, and even as she trembled with a familiar chill, she succumbed quickly to sleep. She reached for her soft quilt and drew it up over her shoulders, trying not to think about how cold she was, trying not to think at all. In fact she shivered so violently she hardly noticed when he sat down, his weight depressing the mattress at the foot of her bed.

Alizeh bit back a scream.

Her eyes flew open, tired pupils fighting to widen their aperture. Frantically, Alizeh patted down her quilt, her pillow, her threadbare mattress. There was no body on her bed. No one in her room.

Had she been hallucinating? She fumbled for her candle

and dropped it, her hands shaking.

Surely, she'd been dreaming.

The mattress groaned—the weight shifting—and Alizeh experienced a fear so violent she saw sparks. She pushed backward, knocking her head against the wall, and somehow the pain focused her panic.

A sharp snap and a flame caught between his barely there fingers, illuminated the contours of his face.

Alizeh dared not breathe.

Even in silhouette she couldn't see him, not properly, but then—it was not his face, but his voice, that had made the devil notorious.

Alizeh knew this better than most.

Seldom did the devil present himself in some approximation of flesh; rare were his clear and memorable communications. Indeed, the creature was not as powerful as his legacy insisted, for he'd been denied the right to speak as another might, doomed forever to hold forth in riddles, and allowed permission only to persuade a person to ruin, never to command.

It was not usual, then, for one to claim an acquaintance with the devil, nor was it with any conviction that a person might speak of his methods, for the presence of such evil was experienced most often only through a provoking of sensation.

Alizeh did not like to be the exception.

Indeed it was with some pain that she acknowledged the circumstances of her birth: that it had been the devil to first offer congratulations at her cradle, his unwelcome ciphers as inescapable as the wet of rain. Alizeh's parents had tried, desperately, to banish such a beast from their home, but he had returned again and again, forever embroidering the tapestry of her life with ominous forebodings, in what seemed a promise of destruction she could not outmaneuver.

Even now she felt the devil's voice, felt it like a breath loosed inside her body, an exhale against her bones.

There once was a man, he whispered.

"No," she nearly shouted, panicking. "Not another riddle—please—"

There once was a man, he whispered, *who bore a snake on each shoulder.*

Alizeh clapped both hands over her ears and shook her head; she'd never wanted so badly to cry.

"Please," she said, "please don't—"

Again:

There once was a man
who bore a snake on each shoulder.
If the snakes were well fed
their master ceased growing older.

Alizeh squeezed her eyes shut, pulled her knees to her chest. He wouldn't stop. She couldn't shut him out.

What they ate no one knew, even as the children—

"Please," she said, begging now. "Please, I don't want to know—"

What they ate no one knew,
even as the children were found
with brains shucked from their skulls,
bodies splayed on the ground.

She inhaled sharply and he was gone, gone, the devil's voice torn free from her bones. The room suddenly shuddered around her, shadows lifting and stretching—and in the warped light a strange, hazy face peered back at her. Alizeh bit her lip so hard she tasted blood.

It was a young man staring at her now, one she did not recognize.

That he was human, Alizeh had no doubt—but something about him seemed different from the others. In the dim light the young man seemed carved not from clay, but marble, his face trapped in hard lines, centered by a soft mouth. The longer she stared at him the harder her heart raced. Was this the man with the snakes? Why did it even matter? Why would she ever believe a single word spoken by the devil?

Ah, but she already knew the answer to the latter.

Alizeh was losing her calm. Her mind screamed at her to look away from the conjured face, screamed that this was all madness—and yet.

Heat crept up her neck.

Alizeh was unaccustomed to staring too long at any face, and this one was violently handsome. He had noble features, all straight lines and hollows, easy arrogance at rest. He tilted his head as he took her in, unflinching as he studied her eyes. All his unwavering attention stoked a forgotten flame inside her, startling her tired mind.

And then, a hand.

His hand, conjured from a curl of darkness. He was looking straight into her eyes when he dragged a vanishing finger across her lips.

She screamed.

KEEP READING FOR A SNEAK PEEK AT

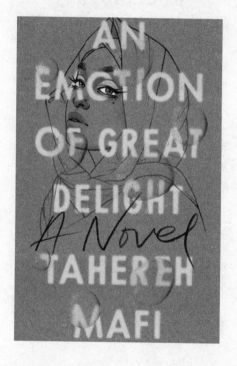

"A bluntly powerful read that shouldn't be missed."
—ALA *Booklist* (starred review)

DECEMBER
2003

ONE

The sunlight was heavy today, fingers of heat forming sweaty hands that braced my face, dared me to flinch. I was stone, still as I stared up into the eye of an unblinking sun, hoping to be blinded. I loved it, loved the blistering heat, loved the way it seared my lips.

It felt good to be touched.

It was a perfect summer day out of place in the fall, the stagnant heat disturbed only by a brief, fragrant breeze I couldn't source. A dog barked; I pitied it. Airplanes droned overhead, and I envied them. Cars rushed by and I heard only their engines, filthy metal bodies leaving their excrement behind and yet—

Deep, I took a deep breath and held it, the smell of diesel in my lungs, on my tongue. It tasted like memory, of movement. Of a promise to go somewhere, I released the breath, anywhere.

I, I was going nowhere.

There was nothing to smile about and still I smiled, the tremble in my lips an almost certain indication of oncoming hysteria. I was comfortably blind now, the sun having burned so deeply into my retinas that I saw little more than glowing orbs, shimmering darkness. I laid backward on dusty asphalt, so hot it stuck to my skin.

I pictured my father again.

His gleaming head, two tufts of dark hair perched atop his ears like poorly placed headphones. His reassuring smile that everything would be fine. The dizzying glare of fluorescent lights.

My father was nearly dead again, but all I could think about was how if he died I didn't know how long I'd have to spend pretending to be sad about it. Or worse, so much worse: how if he died I might not have to pretend to be sad about it. I swallowed back a sudden, unwelcome knot of emotion in my throat. I felt the telltale burn of tears and squeezed my eyes shut, willing myself to get up. Stand up.

Walk.

When I opened my eyes again a ten-thousand-foot-tall police officer was looming over me. Babble on his walkie-talkie. Heavy boots, a metallic swish of something as he adjusted his weight.

I blinked and backed up, crab-like, and evolved from

legless snake to upright human, startled and confused.

"This yours?" he said, holding up a dingy, pale blue back-pack.

"Yes," I said, reaching for it. "Yeah."

He dropped the bag as I touched it, and the weight of it nearly toppled me forward. I'd ditched the bloated carcass for a reason. Among other things, it contained four massive textbooks, three binders, three notebooks, and two worn paper-backs I still had to read for English. The after-school pickup was near a patch of grass I too-optimistically frequented, too often hoping someone in my family would remember I existed and spare me the walk home. Today, no such luck. I'd abandoned the bag and the grass for the empty parking lot.

Static on the walkie-talkie. More voices, garbled.

I looked up.

Up, up a cloven chin and thin lips, nose and sparse lashes, flashes of bright blue eyes. The officer wore a hat. I could not see his hair.

"Got a call," he said, still peering at me. "You go to school here?" A crow swooped low and cawed, minding my business.

"Yeah," I said. My heart had begun to race. "Yes."

He tilted his head at me. "What were you doing on the ground?"

"What?"

"Were you praying or something?"

3

My racing heart began to slow. Sink. I was not devoid of a brain, two eyes, the ability to read the news, a room, this man stripping my face for parts. I knew anger, but fear and I were better acquainted.

"No," I said quietly. "I was just lying in the sun."

The officer didn't seem to buy this. His eyes traveled over my face again, at the scarf I wore around my head. "Aren't you hot in that thing?"

"Right now, yes."

He almost smiled. Instead he turned away, scanned the empty parking lot. "Where are your parents?"

"I don't know."

A single eyebrow went up.

"They forget about me," I said.

Both eyebrows. "They forget about you?"

"I always hope someone will show up," I explained. "If not, I walk home."

The officer looked at me for a long time. Finally, he sighed.

"All right." He backhanded the sky. "All right, get going. But don't do this again," he said sharply. "This is public property. Do your prayers at home."

I was shaking my head. "I wasn't—" I tried to say. *I wasn't*, I wanted to scream. I wasn't.

But he was already walking away.

TWO

It took a full three minutes for the fire in my bones to die out.

In the increasing quiet, I looked up. The once-white clouds had grown fat and gray; the gentle breeze was now a chilling gust. The drunk December day had sobered with a suddenness that bordered on extreme and I frowned at the scene, at its burnt edges, at the crow still circling above my head, its *caw caw* a constant refrain. Thunder roared, suddenly, in the distance.

The officer was mostly memory now.

What was left of him was marching off into the fading light, his boots heavy, his gait uneven; I watched him smile as he murmured into his radio. Lightning tore the sky in two and I shivered, jerkily, as if electrocuted.

I did not have an umbrella.

I reached under my shirt and tugged free the folded

newspaper from where I'd stashed it in my waistband, flush against my torso, and tucked it under my arm. The air was heavy with the promise of a storm, the wind shuddering through the trees. I didn't really think a newspaper would hold up against the rain, but it was all I had.

These days, it was what I always had.

There was a newspaper vending machine around the corner from my house, and a few months ago, on a whim, I'd purchased a copy of the *New York Times*. I'd been curious about Adults Reading the Newspaper, curious about the articles therein that sparked the conversations that seemed to be shaping my life, my identity, the bombing of my friends' families in the Middle East. After two years of panic and mourning post-9/11, our country had decided on aggressive political action: we had declared war on Iraq.

The coverage was relentless.

The television offered a glaring, violent dissemination of information on the subject, the kind I could seldom stomach. But the slow, quiet business of reading a newspaper suited me. Even better, it filled the holes in my free time.

I'd started shoving quarters in my pocket every day, purchasing copies of the newspaper on my way to school. I perused the articles as I walked the single mile, the exercise of mind and body elevating my blood pressure to dangerous heights. By the time I reached first period I'd lost both my appetite and my focus. I was growing sick on the news, sick of it, heedlessly gorging myself on the pain, searching in vain for an antidote in the poison. Even now my thumb moved slowly over the worn ink of old stories, back and forth, caressing my addiction.

I stared up at the sky.

The lone crow overhead would not cease its staring, the weight of its presence seeming to depress the air from my lungs. I forced myself to move, to shutter the windows in my mind as I went. Silence was too welcoming of unwanted thoughts; I listened instead to the sounds of passing cars, to the wind sharpening against their metal bodies. There were two people in particular I did not want to think about. Neither did I want to think about looming college applications, the police officer, or the newspaper still clenched in my fist, and yet—

I stopped, unfurled the paper, smoothed its corners.

Afghan Villagers Torn by Grief After US Raid Kills 9 Children

My phone rang.

I retrieved it from my pocket, going still as I scanned the flashing number on the screen. A blade of feeling impaled me—and then, just as suddenly, withdrew. *Different number.* Heady relief nearly prompted me to laugh, the sensation held at bay only by the dull ache in my chest. It felt as if actual steel had been buried between my lungs.

I flipped open the phone.

"Hello?"

Silence.

A voice finally broke through, a mere half word emerging from a mess of static. I glanced at the screen, at my dying battery, my single bar of reception. When I flipped the phone shut, a prickle of fear moved down my spine.

I thought of my mother.

My mother, my optimistic mother who thought that if she locked herself in her closet I wouldn't hear her sobs.

A single, fat drop of water landed on my head.

I looked up.

I thought of my father, six feet of dying man swaddled in a hospital bed, staring into the middle distance. I thought of my sister.

A second drop of rain fell in my eye.

The sky ruptured with a sudden *crack* and in the intervening second—in the heartbeat before the deluge—I contemplated stillness. I considered lying down in the middle of the road, lying there forever.

But then, rain.

It arrived in a hurry, battering my face, blackening my clothes, pooling in the folds of my backpack. The newspaper I lifted over my head endured all of four seconds before succumbing to the wet, and I hastily tucked it away, this time in my bag. I squinted into the downpour, readjusted the demon on my back, and pulled my thin jacket more tightly around my body.

Walked.

LAST YEAR

PART I

Two sharp knocks at my door and I groaned, pulled the blanket over my head. I'd been up late last night memorizing equations for my physics class, and I'd gotten maybe four hours of sleep as a result. The very idea of getting out of bed made me want to weep.

Another hard knock.

"It's too early," I said, my voice muffled by the blanket. "Go away."

"Pasho," I heard my mother say. *Get up.*

"Nemikham," I called back. *I don't want to.*

"Pasho."

"Actually, I don't think I can go to school today. I think I have tuberculosis."

I heard the soft *shh* of the door pushing open against carpet, and I curled away instinctively, a nautilus in its shell. I

10

made a pitiful sound as I waited for what seemed inevitable—for my mother to drag me, bodily, out of bed, or, at the very least, to rip off the covers.

Instead, she sat on me.

I nearly screamed at the unexpected weight. It was excruciating to be sat upon while curled in the fetal position; somehow my stacked bones made me more vulnerable to damage. I thrashed around, shouted at her to get off me, and she just laughed, pinched my leg.

I cried out.

"Goftam pasho." *I said get up.*

"How am I supposed to get up now?" I asked, batting away the sheets from my face. "You've broken all my bones."

"Eh?" She raised her eyebrows. "You say that to me? Your mother"—she said all this in Farsi—"is so heavy she could break all your bones? Is that what you're saying?"

"Yes."

She gasped, her eyes wide. "Ay, bacheyeh bad." *Oh, you bad child.* And with a slight bounce, she sat more heavily on my thighs.

I let out a strangled cry. "Okay okay I'll get up I'll get up oh my God—"

"Maman? Are you up here?"

At the sound of my sister's voice, my mom got to her feet. She whipped the covers off my bed and said, "In here!" Then, to me, with narrowed eyes: "Pasho."

11

"I'm pasho-ing, I'm pasho-ing," I grumbled.

I got to my feet and glanced, out of habit, at the alarm clock I'd already silenced a half dozen times, and nearly had a stroke when I saw the hour. "I'm going to be late!"

"Man keh behet goftam," my mom said with a shrug. *I told you.*

"You told me nothing." I turned, eyes wide. "You never told me what time it was."

"I did tell you. Maybe your tuberculosis made you deaf."

"Wow." I shook my head as I stalked past her. "Hilarious."

"I know, I know, I'm heelareeus," she said with a flourish of her hand. She switched back to Farsi. "By the way, I can't take you to school today. I have a dentist appointment. Shayda is taking you instead."

"No I'm not," my sister called, her voice growing louder as she approached. She popped her head inside my room. "I have to leave right now, and Shadi isn't even dressed."

"No— Wait—" I startled scrambling. "I can be dressed in five minutes—"

"No you can't."

"Yes I can!" I was already across the hall in our shared bathroom, applying toothpaste to my toothbrush like a crazy person. "Just wait, okay, just—"

"No way. I'm not going to be late because of you."

"Shayda, what the hell—"

"You can walk."

"It'll take me forty-five minutes!"

"Then ask Mehdi."

"Mehdi is still asleep!"

"Did someone say my name?"

I heard my brother coming up the stairs, his words a little rounder than usual, like maybe he was eating something as he spoke. My heart gave a sudden leap.

I spat toothpaste into the sink, ran into the hall. "I need a ride to school," I cried, toothbrush still clenched in my fist. "Can you take me?"

"Never mind. I've gone suddenly deaf." He barreled back down the stairs.

"Oh my God. What is wrong with everyone in this family?"

My dad's voice boomed upward. "Man raftam! Khodafez!" *I'm leaving! Bye!*

"Khodafez!" the four of us shouted in unison.

I heard the front door slam shut as I flew to the banister, caught sight of Mehdi on the landing below.

"Wait," I said, "please, please—"

Mehdi looked up at me and smiled his signature, devastating smile, the kind I knew had already ruined a few lives. His hazel eyes glittered in the early-morning light. "Sorry," he said. "I've got plans."

"How do you have plans at seven thirty in the morning?"

"Sorry," he said again, his lean form disappearing from view. "Busy day."

My mom patted me on the shoulder. "Mikhasti zoodtar pashi." *You could've woken up earlier.*

"An excellent point," Shayda said, swinging her backpack over one shoulder. "Bye."

"No!" I ran back into the bathroom, rinsed my mouth, splashed water on my face. "I'm almost ready! Two more minutes!"

"Shadi, you're not even wearing pants."

"What?" I looked down. I was wearing an oversize T-shirt. No pants. "Wait— Shayda—"

But she was already moving down the stairs.

"Manam bayad beram," my mom said. *I have to go, too.* She shot me a sympathetic glance. "I'll pick you up after school, okay?"

I acknowledged this with a distracted goodbye and darted back into my room. I changed into jeans and a thermal at breakneck speed, nearly stumbling over myself as I grabbed socks, a hair tie, my scarf, and my half-zipped backpack. I flew downstairs like a maniac, screaming Shayda's name.

"Wait," I cried. "Wait, I'm ready! Thirty seconds!"

I hopped on one foot as I pulled on my socks, slipped on my shoes. I tied back my hair, knotted my scarf à la Jackie O— or, you know, a lot of Persian ladies—and bolted out the door. Shayda was at the curb, unlocking her car, and my mom was settling into her minivan, still parked in the driveway. I waved at her, breathless as I shouted—

"I made it!"

My mom smiled and flashed me a thumbs-up, both of which I promptly reciprocated. I then turned the wattage of my smile on Shayda, who only rolled her eyes and, with a heavy sigh, granted me passage in her ancient Toyota Camry.

I was euphoric.

I waved another goodbye at my mom—who'd just turned on her car—before depositing my unwieldy bag in Shayda's back seat. My sister was still buckling herself into the driver's side, arranging her things, placing her coffee mug in the cup holder, et cetera, and I leaned against the passenger side door, taking advantage of the moment to both catch my breath and enjoy my victory.

Too late, I realized I was freezing.

It was the end of September, the beginning of fall, and I hadn't yet adjusted to the new season. The weather was inconsistent, the days plagued by both hot and cold stretches, and I wasn't sure it was worth risking Shayda's wrath to run upstairs and grab my jacket.

My sister seemed to read my mind.

"Hey," she barked at me from inside the car. "Don't even think about it. If you go back in the house, I'm leaving."

My mom, who was also a mind reader, suddenly hit the brakes on her minivan, rolled down the window.

"Bea," she called. *Here.* "Catch."

I held out my hands as she tossed a balled-up sweatshirt in

my direction. I caught it, assessed it, held it up to the sky. It was a standard-issue black hoodie, the kind you pulled over your head. Its only distinguishing features were the drawstrings, which were a vibrant blue.

"Whose is this?" I asked.

My mom shrugged. "It must be Mehdi's," she said in Farsi. "It's been in the car for a long time."

"A long time?" I frowned. "How long is a long time?"

My mom shrugged again, put on her sunglasses.

I gave the cotton a suspicious sniff, but it must not have been abandoned in our car for too long, because the sweater still smelled nice. Something like cologne. Something that made my skin hum with awareness.

My frown deepened.

I pulled the sweatshirt over my head, watched my mom disappear down the drive. The hoodie was soft and warm and way too big for me in the best way, but this close to my skin that faint, pleasant scent was suddenly overwhelming. My thoughts had begun to race, my mind working too hard to answer a simple question.

Shayda honked the horn. I nearly had a heart attack.

"Get in right now," she shouted, "or I'm running you over."

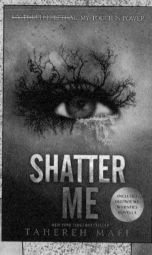

THEIR STORY ISN'T OVER YET.

Return to the world of
SHATTER ME!

Can't get enough of the SHATTER ME series?

SHE WILL CHOOSE ME

DESTROY ME

A SHATTER ME NOVELLA

NEW YORK TIMES BESTSELLING AUTHOR

TAHEREH MAFI

DIGITAL NOVELLA

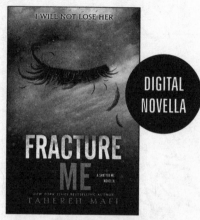

I WILL NOT LOSE HER

FRACTURE ME

A SHATTER ME NOVELLA

NEW YORK TIMES BESTSELLING AUTHOR

TAHEREH MAFI

DIGITAL NOVELLA

HIDING IN PLAIN SIGHT

SHADOW ME

A SHATTER ME NOVELLA

TAHEREH MAFI

DIGITAL NOVELLA

SO MUCH LEFT TO LOSE

REVEAL ME

A SHATTER ME NOVELLA

TAHEREH MAFI

DIGITAL NOVELLA

Read these gripping original novellas in paperback,
UNITE ME and *FIND ME*

Don't miss these stunning novels from the *New York Times* bestselling author of the **SHATTER ME** series.

"The very best books move you to reconsider the world around you, and this is one of those."

—Nicola Yoon, #1 *New York Times* bestselling author

HARPER
An Imprint of HarperCollins*Publishers*

epicreads.com